The Secret Life of Sam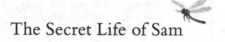

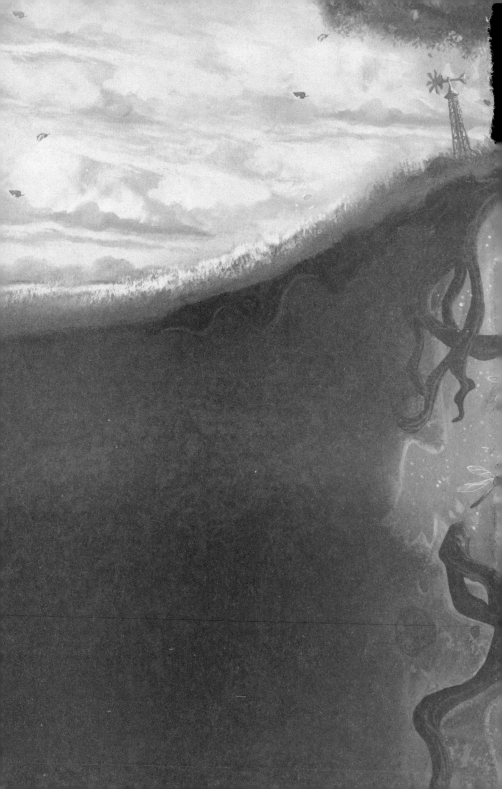

THE SECRET LIFE OF SAM

KIM VENTRELLA

HARPER
An Imprint of HarperCollinsPublishers

Names: Ventrella, Kim, author.
Title: The Secret Life of Sam / Kim Ventrella.
Description: First edition. | New York, NY : HarperCollins, [2020] |
    Audience: Ages 8-12. | Audience: Grades 4-6. | Summary: After his
    father's death, seventh-grader Sam West is whisked from Louisiana to
    Oklahoma, where he discovers a mysterious tree trunk that leads to a
    world where Pa is still alive.
Identifiers: LCCN 2020000846 | ISBN 9780062941183 (hardcover)
Subjects: CYAC: Fathers and sons--Fiction. | Supernatural--Fiction. |
    Aunts--Fiction. | Friendship--Fiction. | Death--Fiction. | Orphans--
    Fiction.
Classification: LCC PZ7.1.V443 Sec 2020 | DDC [Fic]--dc23
LC record available at https://lccn.loc.gov/2020000846

Typography by Chris Kwon
Art by Brandon Dorman
20 21 22 23 24   PC/LSCH   10 9 8 7 6 5 4 3 2 1
❖
First Edition

To all the creators who dare to follow their dreams

1

A DRAGONFLY SETTLED ON THE back of Sam's hand. Pa would have called it good luck. Sam? Not so much. Not anymore. Luck was for other people. People who weren't getting snatched away by some stranger and dragged halfway across the country.

Luck was for people who still had a pa.

Even so, part of him wanted to keep that dragonfly there as long as he could, on the off chance that some of that good luck might rub off. The dragonfly motored its wings, and Sam didn't move an inch, not a muscle. He pretended he was a gator stalking his prey, so still you'd think he was a statue. So still you'd wonder if maybe his scales really had turned to stone.

He looked straight into that dragonfly's shiny, plasticky eyes, daring him to fly away. His legs twitched and his wings gave a flutter.

Sam stopped breathing. This was it. Farewell to his last chance at good luck.

Then the dragonfly's wings settled down, the motor in

his belly slowing to a quiet purr, and Sam could breathe again.

Maybe his luck really was changing for the better.

After all . . .

Pa used to tell a story about how a dragonfly saved him from drowning back in the summer of the big flood. Now *that* was lucky. Pa loved telling stories, even more than fishing or hunting down the Colonel, even more than a warm can of Orange Crush. Although Sam couldn't always tell which stories were true and which were made up.

That year, the Mississippi ran wild, washing away cars and trucks and even entire towns, at least according to Pa. The swamp that wound past the tiny white house on stilts, Sam's swamp, filled up so fast that water spilled in through the doorways and burst out each and every window. Pa had been busy patching up holes when that ornery gator wiggled his way inside.

Sam was a baby back then, but he recalled the story just like he'd really been there. Pa's eyes always got wide when he told the part about fending off that monster gator with nothing but a spatula, his bare hands, and half a roll of duct tape. And all the while, there was baby Sam, snuggled up in an ice cooler on top of the fridge, giggling and clapping his hands.

Pa painted every jaw snap and spatula swipe with words that bloomed in Sam's brain like cherry-red hibiscus flowers unfolding at the first signs of light. Maybe it happened and maybe it didn't, but either way, Sam wanted to believe.

And the story hadn't stopped there. According to Pa, once he had that gator subdued and his jaws taped shut, a wave of water rushed in through an open window, sweeping him off his feet, just like his own personal tsunami. Now, Pa had been a fair swimmer, but he couldn't have counted on falling and conking his head on the corner of his tackle box. That blow knocked him out clean, and he would have drowned for sure if a dragonfly hadn't come along at that exact moment to revive him. To hear Pa tell it, that dragonfly landed square between his eyes, buzzing and twitching and running his motor, and not stopping until Pa woke up sputtering. Pa was so relieved to be alive that he gave that dragonfly a wet kiss on the lips before grabbing baby Sam and retreating to the roof to keep from drowning.

That dragonfly had been a miracle. A godsend. A big fat megadose of good luck.

Sam didn't believe that Pa had actually kissed the dragonfly on the lips, not really, but he believed the rest of it. Maybe even the part about dragonflies being good luck. A little bit. Sort of.

Okay, not so much.

He let out his breath nice and slow so as not to startle the dragonfly and then drew in a bellyful of fresh air. The dragonfly shifted again and twittered its wings, but didn't fly away.

He looked out at the misty swamp that snaked around the tiny white house on stilts like a cottonmouth squeezing its prey. Shimmery blue-and-green dragonflies danced on the still water, touching down just long enough to wet their toes. Pa always said they reminded him of tiny helicopters dropping in to deliver supplies, but Sam thought they looked more like ghosts. Especially when the light was just right and their wings glowed like clear sheets of paper ringed with spidery bones.

He listened to the water lapping at the wooden poles that held up the dock. Once in a while, it reached so high that it tickled the tips of his sneakers, which were currently dangling off the edge. He imagined Pa beside him, holding his fishing rod, just like this was any other day and not Sam's last. He touched the can of Orange Crush sitting next to him, in honor of Pa, but didn't take a drink. He hadn't even opened it.

After a while, he closed his eyes. Behind his eyelids, he saw swamp monsters licking the poles clean with their long, slimy tongues. He saw the ghost of Saint George himself—as in Bayou St. George, the name of his hometown—battling a dragon with three heads and rusty nails for teeth. He saw all the larger-than-life moments from Pa's stories swirling in the murky water, sinking deeper and deeper into the shadows, and he saw Pa holding a flashlight to his face, eyes sparkling with mischief.

Would he still see Pa when his grape-soda aunt drove him to a grape-soda city in a whole other grape-soda state? (*Grape soda* was the word Pa always used when Sam was around and he was trying not to cuss, since grape soda was the Voldemort of the soda world and the archnemesis of his favorite soda, Orange Crush.)

Would he still remember Pa's stories? Would he close his eyes and see his face?

He thought back to all those nights sitting on the dock with Pa, watching the lightning bugs twinkle over the green, glassy water. Sam fishing or doing his homework, Pa scribbling down stories in one of his beat-up notebooks. Sam wished he could go back and make those nights stretch on forever. Just him and Pa and an entire case of Orange Crush. Pa liked it warm, because he said it tasted like syrup, and Sam liked listening to Pa's stories that continued on long into the night, and he liked the chorus of bullfrogs and cicadas that served as accompaniment, and he even liked a warm Orange Crush from time to time, even though to him tasting like syrup wasn't all that great.

Every once in a while, when Pa was regaling Sam with yet another tale, he'd pass the flashlight over and say, "Go on. You finish it." And he'd offer up his famous gator smile. He called it his gator smile because he'd gotten his two front teeth knocked out by a baby gator back when he used to run boat tours up and down the swamp. Those were different from his other missing teeth, which were down to Bobby Joe's pet raccoon.

"You can do it. Use your imagination," Pa would say, and so Sam would take the flashlight and shine it on his face, but no matter how hard he tried he could never find the words to make a good story. He was better at sitting back and listening than coming up with the words himself.

He let out another breath and the dragonfly shivered on his arm but, believe it or not, it still didn't let go. He wondered how long it would hang on before it got an itch and decided to fly away back home.

Was it really passing on some much-needed good luck?

Maybe.

About time.

Probably not.

But Pa would say it was, otherwise why would it stay on his arm so long? Sam wanted to believe, but another part of him, the bigger part, thought that his luck had died right along with Pa. Pa was the one who could weave magic out of thin air, with nothing in his belly but cheese curls and orange soda. He was the one who'd survived a flood, a bear attack, and a whole slew of hungry gators, not to mention the time he'd wrestled an escaped warthog and lived to tell the tale.

So many adventures, but in the end, none of it mattered. Luck wasn't magic after all. It was made up, just like Pa's stories.

That's the truth that everybody was afraid to tell him: Bobby Joe from the tackle shop, Miss Sara Reed from the feed store, their closest neighbors, even mean old Aunt Jo who'd come down from Nowhere, Oklahoma, to take him away. Pa was gone and that was that. He wasn't in a better place, sitting on clouds singing with some grape-soda angels. He wasn't battling gators forever in his own private heaven or tumbling through a mystical forest, grabbing a giant warthog by the horns. He was gone. It didn't matter how you said it.

Real life was 99.9 percent grape-flavored and only the tiniest bit orange. Luck wasn't real, and neither was heaven or any of it.

Pa was dead and buried.

Story over.

The end.

Just then, the April sun peeked through the treetops and hit Sam straight in the face. He blinked away the burn, and when his vision came back, the world appeared in slices, each one bathed in that grape-soda light: the cascades of Spanish moss spilling from the tupelo branches, weighing them down like crooked old men. The patched-up rowboat that Pa had made himself and the sign that Aunt Jo had just taped to the prow: *Free to good home*. The trail of a gator cutting a winding path through the water, Pa's beer-can wind chimes clanking angrily in the breeze, the model plane Pa had ordered from a catalog that they'd built together, sitting by Sam's side, the propeller spinning listlessly round and round.

He saw all of it, but in a way he didn't see any of it. Just looking at it stung his eyes, even after the glare of the sun faded. How could you look at something that you'd always known, that you thought would be there even when you got old and wrinkled and had to use a stick just to stay upright? How could you look out at all that knowing it would be the very last time?

"Ouch!"

The dragonfly dug its front toes into Sam's skin, wings buzzing to life.

"Wait!" Sam said, but the dragonfly didn't listen. With another pinch, it launched skyward, hovering higher and higher before swooping down after some unsuspecting mosquito.

That's luck for you. Just some bug that leaves the second it gets bored. Sam watched its shimmering body dance along the surface of the water with the others, searching for food. Soon he couldn't tell one dragonfly from another.

WITH THAT UGLY OLD INSECT gone, Sam couldn't stand to look out at Ol' Tired Eyes for one more second. That was Pa's name for the swamp, since he said the pool of green glass reminded him of a misty-eyed giant who got buried in an earthquake and spent his days staring up at the sun. Everything about the swamp and the tiny white house on stilts and even the hot, muggy air made Sam feel like he needed to escape. It was like how Pa didn't keep any pictures of Mama in his room, since looking at them made his heart ache.

Sam thought about leaving the De Havilland Mosquito bomber to the rain and the gators. That was the name of the model plane he and Pa had built together. It was a two-seater flown by British pilots during World War II, and it was unusual since it had been made almost entirely of wood.

Grape-soda plane.

Pointless piece of wood.

Might as well let it rot away like the rest of Pa's stuff.

His knees cracked as he got up, leaving the plane sitting there on the edge of the dock, next to the untouched can of Orange Crush. He opened the screen door and held it there, sweat dripping down his back. What use was a toy plane now that he didn't have anyone to fly it with? He opened the main door, feeling the whoosh of air-conditioning on his face. But then he let both doors swing shut again. He couldn't leave it.

True, the plane reminded him of Pa in the worst possible way. It even smelled like him, tool grease and chewing tobacco, but then he thought about how Pa had saved up for two months to buy it, working extra shifts at the feed store when Sam thought he was up at the Gator Shack watching the game. He walked back and picked up the De Havilland, careful not to get a dirt smudge on her metallic silver paint, and then he hurried inside without another look behind him. He slammed the screen door and then the regular door, turning the rusty dead bolt.

He left the can of Orange Crush behind. For Pa. Though it wasn't like he could ever drink it.

Whatever.

Oh well.

What did he care?

He was almost grateful when Aunt Jo came huffing up the basement steps carrying two boxes, one balanced on top of the other, because it meant he didn't have to think about

the grape-soda swamp and how he'd just looked out at Ol'
Tired Eyes for the last time.

"This is all that's left," she said, dropping the boxes
unceremoniously on the empty living room floor and
adjusting her artificial leg. He heard glass Christmas orna-
ments crunching, but told himself it didn't bother him. It
was better this way. "You wanna look through these boxes
before I load 'em up?"

Sam took a quick look at Pa's handwriting on the side of
the box, sloppy as usual but with big, swirly tails for the *Y*
and the *S*: *Our Fancy Christmas*.

"No," Sam said. He looked away, blinking his grape-
soda eyes, and he decided to wait out on the porch where
nobody was staring at him like he was some pathetic lost
puppy with a smashed paw. Aunt Jo wasn't good at much as
far as he could tell, except for staring and breaking things,
and he didn't care to stick around to witness either.

He sat there on the porch like a Christmas statue, like
the ugly figurine of Joseph dressed in fishing gear that Pa
had bought one year at the feed store, only that was probably broken now too. He watched as Aunt Jo stomped across
the dirt, heaving the Christmas boxes into the giant gray
dumpster like it was nothing. When the boxes hit the bottom they must have activated Pa's Big Mouth Bass, because
Sam heard grainy music and a croaky voice belting out
"Foggy Bottom Blues." He closed his eyes, wishing he had

his earbuds and some dark glasses to block out all the sun.

But he didn't have his earbuds, and so he listened as Aunt Jo loaded up the rest of their things, her old lady shoes crunching on the gravel.

"Need to make a pit stop before we go?" she said. Sam could feel her shadow stretching over him, just like one of Pa's swamp monsters, only worse because she smelled like chewing gum and Aspercreme, which was a grape-soda way to smell for a monster. He didn't answer. "Suit yourself. Next stop's not for sixty miles. Hope you know how to pee in a bottle."

Sam said nothing, and he didn't open his eyes until he heard Aunt Jo turn the key in the front door for the very last time.

"I guess that's that," she said, staring at the dirty white door that still had Sam's faded Halloween decorations stuck on with strips of duct tape, even all these months later. Aunt Jo gave the door a rough pat, her square jaws pinched. She held her hand there for a while, like it was Pa she was touching, not a slab of wood with peeling paint, and then she spun on her heels and pummeled the gravel all the way to the car. She stopped once, grimacing like she'd just stepped on a nail, then she shook it off and kept right on going.

The car was a 1962 VW Bug with the words *Baby Girl* painted on the side in sparkly green paint. It was nothing compared to Pa's '68 Sunbird, but Aunt Jo talked like it was something special. She liked to say that she won Baby Girl in a snake-rustling contest as a girl.

But that was before.

When she was still the other Aunt Jo and not some stranger.

"What's snake rustling?" Sam had said one Thanksgiving back when he was seven or eight and Aunt Jo was still Aunt Jo. He remembered sitting on a stool in the kitchen back in the day, watching Aunt Jo clean gizzards out of the Thanksgiving turkey, her strong hands slick with innards.

She raised one burly eyebrow and sucked her lips at him. "What's that brother of mine been teaching you? Next you'll be telling me you don't know a croc from a gator."

"I do so!" Sam had said, his hackles rising at the insult.

"Then you ought to know about snake rustling." She shook her finger at him and a bit of turkey gut flew off and landed on the kitchen counter. "It's a hunt. Every year, people from all around Oklahoma come to hunt snakes and toss 'em in this big pit just off the highway. There's a trophy in it for the one who catches the most, and Pops, that's your granddad, bet me Ma's old car I couldn't catch a single one. Ends up, I caught more than the three biggest men combined, and I got a car that day to boot."

Sam had been impressed, though he hadn't shown it.

Now he looked at the green, slithery letters that spelled out *Baby Girl* and he wished that Aunt Jo had stayed away, just like she had the past four Thanksgivings. Not a single phone call. Not even a card.

Without another word, she got in the driver's seat and started up the car, the engine growling like an angry gator. Sam's stuff was already in the trunk—a backpack and a beat-up suitcase that used to belong to Pa. He wondered what would happen if he just sat there on the porch steps and refused to get up. Aunt Jo might be strong—even though she was the baby sister, she looked like a linebacker compared to his scrawny Pa—but that didn't mean she was prepared to carry him. And she sure couldn't catch him.

He could see her watching him through the dusty windshield. The sun glared off her glasses and sparkled in her gray, cropped hair. Why couldn't she have just stayed away? Who was she to throw all of Pa's stuff in a dumpster like it was garbage? Like his whole life was something you could just get rid of, same as the broken TVs and microwaves people were always leaving on the side of the road?

And who was she to come back after all these years telling him what to do and where to go and saying that Pa was in a better place now and that this is what he would have wanted? What the heck did she know about what he wanted? Just because he wrote it down on some grape-soda piece of paper saying that Aunt Jo was in charge didn't make it true. She didn't belong here. She was nobody to Pa. A stranger.

Aunt Jo revved the engine. The Big Mouth Bass started singing again, its death rattle echoing against the walls of the dumpster. Sam watched Baby Girl rumbling in the same patch of grass where Pa always parked, and he couldn't help thinking of the Sunbird sitting in a junkyard somewhere, the front end a tangle of ugly, twisted metal.

Something inside Sam snapped.

He shot up, the De Havilland bomber tumbling from his lap, and made a beeline for the gray dumpster taking up half the yard. It looked like the back of a semitruck, only the top was open and it didn't have any wheels. He started kicking it first, his sneakers clanging and vibrating against the metal. Then kicking wasn't enough and he started punching, and then, when his knuckles hurt too bad to keep it up, he slapped it over and over with his open palm. Then with both palms.

The whole time, Aunt Jo waited in the car, the engine idling and pumping out smoke. Sam's toes and hands and arms ached, but it was like the feeling you got after staying out too long in the cold. They hurt deep down, but on the surface he didn't feel anything, despite the blood trickling over his torn-up knuckles. He stood there for a long while, thinking how he should run away and where he would hide and how he'd come back out of the woods when the garbage men came to protect all of Pa's things.

But he didn't run away.

The car grumbled and popped, and inside Aunt Jo stayed quiet. The muggy breeze dried his bloody hands, and he could hear Pa's beer-can wind chimes clinking all the way from the back deck. He didn't know why he did it, not exactly, but he went back to the porch and picked up his plane. Two of the propeller blades had snapped, and a crack ran up the left wing. He slid the broken blades into his pocket and climbed into the car.

It smelled like pine air freshener and Aspercreme and old Kleenexes. It smelled like a coffin filled with old bones and dead air. He settled the plane on his lap. The hinges squeaked as he slammed the car door with a hollow thud. He didn't look at Aunt Jo, and she didn't say a word as she put the car in reverse and then started the slow grind down the long, narrow driveway.

Once they reached the smooth asphalt of Route 4, Aunt Jo switched on the radio. Instead of normal music, an airy voice crackled from the ancient speakers.

"You are enough. Spread out your arms and embrace the universe. You are worth rooting for." Behind the airy voice, ocean waves crashed.

"Hope you don't mind," Aunt Jo said, tapping the

stereo that, seriously, had an actual cassette player. "It's my positive-affirmations tape. Thought it might be good for the drive."

Great. Sam rolled down his window using the rusty crank, but it would only go halfway. Whatever. At least it let in the humid air and drowned out the annoying positive affirmations, whatever the heck those were.

They drove for hours on a two-lane road surrounded by wild, stooped-over trees. His cheeks grew red and raw from the wind and his eyes stung like sandpaper, but he refused to roll up the window. At least this way he didn't feel so trapped. At least this way he didn't have to think about Pa and the Sunbird and the way he must have felt on his last ride.

"Your pa grew up in Holler," Aunt Jo said, turning down the tape and speaking loud so her voice carried over the wind. "He ever tell you that? Back then it was me and your pa against the world. People couldn't believe we weren't twins, even though I was a year younger and a foot taller. That's 'cause we were both what people called wayward souls. When we weren't getting into trouble, you could be sure we were plotting and planning."

Sam looked over just long enough to see Aunt Jo studying him out of the side of her eye. He turned back to face the window.

"We were supposed to head out together, the day after

my graduation. Our next big adventure. Save up enough to buy a car and then drive out to LA or New York City and see where the road took us. Then I won Baby Girl, and all that changed. Your pa never had been any good at waiting."

Sam sat there wishing she'd hurry up and finish her story, get it over with already, but she drove on in silence. Probably this was part of some secret plan to get him talking, but he didn't care. So what if he talked? That didn't mean she won. Besides, where did she get off accusing his pa of being impatient?

"So what happened?"

Aunt Jo sucked in a deep breath and let it out again, giving Baby Girl's dashboard a pat. "Your pa took off in Baby Girl first chance he got. I woke up one morning and found a note taped to the garage. 'Sorry, Jojo. Got itchy feet. See you at Thanksgiving.' And he was true to his word. Three months later he showed up on the doorstep like nothing ever happened. Got this paint job done up and everything, as a way to make it up to me, but Pops was spitting fire."

"Where'd he go?" Sam said. He had more questions, too, but each word was like a rock scraping its way up his throat.

"How should I know? But that's your pa for you. Always chasing after something. Same happened the summer he had you. Quit a perfectly good job at the gator farm to go off wandering around the mountains. How he came back with a baby in three months' time, God only knows, but there you were."

"And Ma?"

Aunt Jo got quiet. The car slowed and then sped up again as she shifted in her seat. Sam already knew part of the story. That Pa had fallen in love up on that mountain, and that he wasn't Sam's real dad, at least not in the biological sense, but that had never mattered a lick to either of them. Sam also knew that Mama had died when Sam was young, too young to remember her, except for what he'd seen in pictures. And whenever he asked how Mama died, Pa would clam right up, like someone had sealed his lips with a strip of duct tape.

"What'd he tell you about her?"

Sam watched Aunt Jo with her bulky, awkward shoulders, her droopy elbows and thin, chapped lips. True, they were family, but she was a stranger to him too. A face he hadn't seen in so long he'd just about forgotten it, not all that different from Mama.

"I want you to tell me."

He could see her thinking it over, her jaw bones working back and forth beneath her skin. They passed a billboard for Big Al's BBQ Shack and Gator Farm, and Aunt Jo yawned. "Pit stop up ahead. Don't know about you, but I could use a snack."

Sam just stared at her, but Aunt Jo kept on driving like

she didn't even see him. Like she could erase his words with a yawn and an offer of snacks. Well, two could play at that game.

They ate in silence at Al's BBQ Shack, sitting in a sticky vinyl booth by the window. Every time Sam went to swallow, it felt like he was forcing down a mouthful of rocks. He left most of his ribs on his plate and then went out to the car while Aunt Jo waited for a to-go box.

Neither of them spoke at all after that, except Aunt Jo, who said, "Go buggy," and punched the roof of the car every time they passed another VW Bug. Most of the time, when he looked over, she had one hand on the steering wheel and the other on this ugly poker chip she wore on a chain around her neck. As they headed out of Louisiana into Texas, Aunt Jo finally switched to talk radio for a while, until the voices got all choppy and turned to static. Aunt Jo didn't seem to notice.

About eight hours into their drive, they crossed the Red River into Oklahoma. As soon as they did, the wind picked up and rattled the half-open window like an invisible tornado. Sam stuck his head into the wind tunnel and let the drone fill up his ears and shake loose his dark thoughts.

Something about that wind shook loose more than his thoughts too. The back of his throat got tight, and heat surged into his cheeks. The next thing he knew his face was

20

throbbing and wet, just like some little crybaby.

Aunt Jo turned off the radio, but he couldn't stop the tears from coming—like one grape-soda earthquake after another, they shook his entire body in waves. He felt the car slow down and then bump its way onto the shoulder. Aunt Jo put the car in park. He wished she'd turn the radio back on or say something, but she just sat there.

After a while she rested a heavy hand on his shoulder. The weight of it helped to steady his breathing, and the waves smoothed out and his body went quiet. He sat there feeling like an old rag left out in the rain and wondering how his cheeks could ache so bad after only one round of tears. Once again, he was glad for the open window and the dry, hot gusts whipping past his face.

"Your pa loved you, more than you could know." Aunt Jo gave his shoulder a squeeze and let go. "And he was proud of you. I know I haven't been around, not like I should." Her voice grew tight, like maybe she was a big crybaby just like Sam. "But I can tell you that much."

Sam didn't know what to say to that since they were just words and didn't change anything, but some of the anger in his heart had drained away, and when Aunt Jo pulled back onto the highway, she switched the radio on and turned it to some real music. Twangy bluegrass, just like Pa would have liked.

It turned out that Oklahoma looked a lot like Louisiana, only if you emptied out all the trees and flattened out the hills until all you had were wide-open fields and dead grass. Sam wondered if they had any gators, or for that matter, any swamps.

"Not long now," Aunt Jo said as they bumped over a set of railroad tracks.

Sam watched out the window as fields of wheat and corn flitted past, broken up by the occasional electrical-power plant.

"Sign's up ahead." Aunt Jo slowed down as they passed a hand-painted sign: *Welcome to Holler, Oklahoma*, only the letters were so worn and faded that all he could see were gray ghosts where the words should have been. The road turned from asphalt to gravel and the vibration made Sam's teeth clack. Off to his right, he saw what looked like a Greek ruin complete with ivory columns sitting alone in a sea of overgrown grass.

"That used to be the train depot," Aunt Jo said, her face splitting into a smile. "Your pa and I would play invaders out there. He was the Trojan army and I was Odysseus, leader of the Greeks." When she smiled, she almost looked like the Aunt Jo he remembered. Almost.

Sam tried to imagine his pa running through the overgrown fields as a boy or climbing up the crumbling

22

columns, but he couldn't.

"School's not far," Aunt Jo said as they drove up a hill and came upon the first trees he'd seen in just about forever. The dusty clock on the dash read 3:45 p.m. Aunt Jo kept on talking, but Sam was no longer listening. According to the article in the paper the next day, that had been the time of Pa's accident. Aunt Jo's words turned to an angry buzzing in his head. What were the chances they'd arrive at the same time Pa died? The heat wrapped around him, squeezing his chest, like he was a mummy in a coffin, only they'd accidentally buried him alive. He had to get out of the car. He had to—

A loud pop interrupted his panic. Next thing he knew, the front tire was sending up smoke that streamed in through the open window and worked its way down Sam's throat.

Aunt Jo pulled over and they both stumbled from the car, choking.

"Mother, Mary, and Joseph," Aunt Jo said, bending down to look at the flat tire. Half a broken bottle had sliced into the rubber, tearing a hole the size of a fist. Aunt Jo had some choice words for that bottle, a few Sam hadn't heard before, but Sam was almost happy. As Aunt Jo dug the spare tire out of the trunk and set to prying off the old one, all he could think was that he was glad to be out of that grape-soda car, where he could breathe again.

23

"Your pa ever teach you how to change a spare?" Aunt Jo said, her butt waving in the air as she worked to loosen the rusty lug nut. "'Course, he was always more interested in fishing than helping Pops and me out in the shop. Did he ever tell you about that time he left the cap off a leaky radiator and . . ."

Sam walked away and let the whipping wind eat up Aunt Jo's words. Pa was a better mechanic than she'd ever be, even if he did prefer fishing. He'd fixed up his '68 Pontiac Sunbird all by himself, hadn't he? Well, with Sam's help, and it had been good as new before . . . Dang! Why did his brain have to keep going back to the accident? And where did Aunt Jo get off calling his pa lazy and ignorant? Especially right now. 3:45 p.m. Hadn't anyone ever taught her about respecting the dead?

He headed up the road a bit, the school a collection of gray, squat buildings in the distance, until he came to a single scraggly tree. Unlike the other trees closer to the car, this one looked half-dead and rotten. He didn't usually get carsick but something about being trapped inside Baby Girl and the dry, whipping wind and the field of dead grass that didn't look anything like Ol' Tired Eyes made his stomach churn. He felt like he was all dried out inside and no matter how much water he poured down his gullet he'd never get back to normal again.

It was one thing driving away from the swamp and the

24

tiny house in Bayou St. George; it was another standing here in grape-soda Holler, Oklahoma, while the wind kicked up a cloud of white dust. Maybe it was just that all the moisture had been sucked out of the air, or maybe it was the sea of tangled grass grabbing at his legs or the rattling of dead branches, but either way, he couldn't stand to look at Aunt Jo or listen to her stories or ride in her coffin of a car for one more second.

Truth was, he didn't want to hear another word about Pa just now. He was here and Pa was there, dead and buried. And even if his spirit stuck around like some people thought, then how could it find him all the way out here in a town so small no one even bothered to paint the sign?

Besides, Sam didn't believe in ghosts. That was Pa's thing, ghosts and will-o'-the-wisps and dragonflies that brought seven years' good luck. Pa could believe in just about anything, and he was always clipping articles from sketchy tabloids about swamp monsters or planes that went missing and were never found.

Sam didn't believe in any of that. He didn't even believe in heaven and hell when it came right down to it, which meant his pa wasn't anywhere, not back home and not here. He was gone. Just a bunch of dry bones and white dust.

The wind whistled inside the hollowed-out tree.

It went in hot and dry and came out cool. Sam stepped closer, shaking all the grape-soda thoughts from his brain, and ran his fingers along the hole in the tree. The hole was deep and dark, like someone had scooped away the insides of a pumpkin and left nothing behind but jagged scars. He leaned in, pressing his face into the cool darkness, and it smelled like that time Pa had taken him down into Wolf Rock Cave: wet and old and vast.

He closed his eyes and thought he heard water dripping somewhere in the distance. He leaned in deeper still, the gentle pressure of the shadows sending a shiver through his skin. As the darkness closed around him, the rest of the world faded away—Holler, Aunt Jo and her grape-soda car, the dumpster full of Pa's things, the Big Mouth Bass still singing somewhere under all that trash.

A bead of moisture trickled down his forehead. Somewhere below, a small, insignificant voice was calling his name. He pressed in deeper. A waxy leaf touched his cheek, a trail of wet moss. He coiled his fingers into the cool wetness, pulling himself forward. For a moment, his body tipped forward and it was like he was teetering on the edge of a cliff, but then a weight slammed into his shin and he pulled back. His head cracked into the bark on the way out, and he fell, butt-first, to the hard-packed earth.

When he looked up, he saw a cat poised between his feet, head tilted to the side, appraising him with one silver eye. The other eye—in fact, the entire other side of his face—looked like it had been smashed in and then sewn back together again. Where his ear and eye socket should have been were lumps of puckered skin covered in mottled gray fur. He was by far the ugliest cat Sam had ever seen, with a bony back that twisted to the left and sharp hip bones that stuck out on either side of a long, bottle-brush tail.

The strange thing was that the cat seemed familiar somehow, though Sam couldn't say from where. The cat stretched, arching his back and licking his needle-thin claws. The wind died down, the skeletal branches settling into place, and suddenly Aunt Jo's voice cut through the silence.

"Did you hear me? Tire's fixed! We're good to go!"

"Coming," he said, but he never took his eyes off the cat. He watched as it leaped into the hollow of the tree, the same hollow that seemed to be watching him like a great, gaping eye. The cat glared back, his single eye sparkling, his lips curling into a strange, saturnine grin. A rush of fear coursed through Sam, like icy fingernails trailing down his back.

Then the cat turned, slashing his tail at the air, and disappeared into the blackness of the hollow.

For a moment, Sam couldn't move. The wind picked up again, and suddenly he could hear the dying cries of the Big Mouth Bass as it sang its final notes, trapped inside its metal prison. 3:45 p.m., though it must be later now. Still, he could hear radio static and beer-can chimes and a voice from the tape deck telling him, "Every day is a new tomorrow."

Fingers numb, he stood and peered inside the tree. Where could the cat have gone? He searched for signs of the strange creature, the hint of a silvery eye, a hank of matted gray fur. The hollow was empty. He leaned closer. Inside the cavity, sunlight cast acorn shells and dead leaves in a soft, golden glow. He touched a brittle stem, a gum wrapper, a piece of dry bark.

No cat.

3

SAM JUMPED AS A BUZZING something landed on the back of his neck. He swatted at his invisible attacker, wondering if the cat had somehow leaped down on him from above. But it wasn't the cat.

It was a dragonfly.

He looked down at its broken body twitching in the dirt.

"What in gravy's name?" Aunt Jo came up behind him, leaning down to examine the insect. "Haven't seen one of those around in, well, just about forever. It's too dry out here. Ain't that something."

They both watched as the dragonfly gave one final twitch and then went still. Sam's stomach clenched. Now he really was gonna be sick. What was a dragonfly doing here in Holler, Oklahoma, and why'd he have to be the one to kill it?

He was heading back toward the car, wallowing in his bad luck, when Aunt Jo yelped. He turned and watched in amazement as the dragonfly, the one he'd just smashed to death, motored straight for Aunt Jo's face before changing direction and zipping up past her ear, into the dead branches. Sam tried to follow its flight, but the glare of the sun blocked his view.

"Imagine that," Aunt Jo said, once she'd calmed down enough to catch her breath. "A dragonfly in these parts. I wonder if he hitched a ride from the bayou."

Sam was wondering that too.

Aunt Jo peeked into the hollow of the tree and then came back up shaking her head. "Oh well, what would life be without a little mystery? That's what your pa used to say." She gave Sam a pat on the shoulder that almost knocked him to his knees. "Come on, we'll drive past the school and then grab some food on our way to the house. You hungry? Gina's Diner makes a chicken-fried steak as big as your head, and it's free if you eat it in under forty-five minutes."

"I'm not hungry."

"Suit yourself." She tried to give his shoulder a squeeze, but he shrugged free from her grip and headed back toward the car.

By the time Aunt Jo got in, Sam was already sitting on his side, cheek pressed against the half-open window.

"Everything all right? You feel carsick?" she said.

"No."

"Headache?"

"No."

"Anything you want to talk about?"

Sam swallowed. What could he say? That he didn't want to be here. That she was some stranger and he planned to run away the first chance he got or report her for kidnapping. That maybe he was losing it, because he'd just seen a cat disappear into thin air and what did it even matter? Grape-soda Holler, Oklahoma. Grape-soda cat.

"No."

Sam waited for Aunt Jo to start the car and stop looking at him like she expected a different answer. Finally the engine rumbled to life, sending a fresh wave of vibrations up his backside. He relaxed a little once they started moving. He was still trapped, but at least he wasn't standing still.

As they passed the tree, Sam searched for signs of the cat or the dragonfly, but didn't see any. He tried to remember where he could have seen the cat before, with its face all smashed in and healed over, but his mind had gone blank.

Aunt Jo started telling stories again as they passed the school, but Sam didn't listen. It wasn't that he was trying to be a jerk, just that his head would probably explode if he heard one more word. Especially since all of Aunt Jo's stories had to do with Pa, and she kept talking about him like he was hers and not just some guy she hadn't seen or called for the past four years, even last Christmas when Pa's leg nearly got run over by a lawn mower.

"Chicken-fried steak or meat-loaf special?" she said.

Sam looked up and realized that they had pulled to a stop

31

in front of a dumpy-looking diner with cinder-block walls and an old ice machine beside the doors pumping out gray smoke.

"Neither."

"I'll get you the lasagna, then, but fair warning: it tastes like sweaty cheese and week-old hot dogs."

"Fine."

Aunt Jo lingered like she was waiting for him to change his mind, but he didn't, and finally she left him alone and went inside. He watched out the window as this dad tried to get his kid to put on a seat belt, but the kid kept kicking the back of the seat and refusing to do it, and then finally the dad gave up and drove off anyway, even though that kid was just one big windshield splat waiting to happen.

When Aunt Jo came back, the whole car filled up with this sweaty-hotdog-cheese smell. She'd ordered him a soda too, a Sprite even though he only drank Orange Crush, but he didn't say anything because his throat was still scratchy from the wind and, besides, he wasn't thirsty.

"This is it," Aunt Jo said when they pulled up to a big two-story house painted Easter-egg yellow. It had these little towers that reminded Sam of a doll's house, but he couldn't picture Aunt Jo living inside since he was pretty sure she'd never played with dolls.

She turned off the engine and they sat in the car swimming in a fog of barfy lasagna scent. "Welcome home,"

Aunt Jo said, and her voice had this grape-soda wobble, and Sam turned to look at her like she'd sprouted tentacles from her eye sockets.

"This isn't my home."

"No," she said, and she didn't even argue, but just sat there, taking a bunch of deep breaths instead. "You come inside when you're ready."

He could feel her looking at his face and he wished she'd stop and go away, and finally she did. He opened his door to let out some of the lasagna stink that lingered even though Aunt Jo had taken the Styrofoam boxes inside. He didn't actually want to be mean to Aunt Jo or call her a monster, even in his head, but she really was a monster if she thought he could ever see this place as home.

He kicked the dashboard and the glove compartment opened, and he found an old pack of Kleenexes with the edges turned yellow and a small plastic photo album with pictures of Pa and Aunt Jo and Pops and some with Sam as a baby. He flipped through them, except the pages were so old that the plastic stuck together and he had to peel them apart like slices of American cheese.

The more he flipped through the pictures, the more they started to make him mad. Who was Aunt Jo to keep pictures of him and Pa? Just some weird lady who never answered her phone or came to visit, and so why keep pictures anyway? Probably so she could show them off to all her made-up friends and pretend like she had a family when she really didn't. Family came home for Thanksgiving and Christmas, and they answered the phone when your dad got his foot run over by a riding lawn mower and you didn't know what to do since all you got when you dialed 911 was a busy signal.

It was dark by the time Sam finally went inside the house.

The dollhouse looked like this: an entryway with an ugly glass table, mail stacked neatly in one corner, numbered keys hanging on hooks. A living room on the right that was bigger than Sam's whole house but with crappy furniture: an army-green sofa with the stuffing coming out, a coffee table, a TV tray on either end of the couch but no TV, a wall of dusty bookshelves, a piano with newspapers stacked on the keys, pictures of Pops and Pa and Sam, pictures of Aunt Jo in her army uniform, a glass cabinet filled with fat baby figurines, angels, and a bunch of grape-soda Jesus statues, a whole lot of empty space. A kitchen on the left: vinyl flooring peeling up at the edges, a stained countertop, a round table with a plastic sunflower tablecloth, more pictures on the fridge.

Aunt Jo was standing at the sink clinking dishes. Sam stood in the hallway that separated the kitchen from the living room and watched her scrub meat-loaf juice off a yellow plate.

"Food's in the oven," she said without turning around,

but Sam didn't move because he wasn't hungry and he didn't want to give Aunt Jo the satisfaction.

She finished cleaning the plate and put it in the drying rack, and then she walked right past him back into the living room. It turned out she did have a TV, except he hadn't recognized it because it was the kind that looked like a big wooden box and besides it had been covered by another ugly tablecloth. She peeled back the tablecloth and settled down on the green couch. It squeaked like a dead pig when she sat on it. She turned on the fishing channel, which was also Pa's favorite, and Sam stood there in the space between the kitchen and the living room feeling like an alien in the world's ugliest dollhouse.

He waited for the commercials to come on, and then the next round of commercials, and finally he decided that maybe he was hungry after all and anyway he wasn't going to let Aunt Jo stop him from eating. He opened up the oven and breathed in the scent of warm hot dogs and sweaty cheese. The smell awakened the feeling he'd had on the car ride up here, like his brain was stuffed full of tissues and he would maybe barf if he didn't get some air.

Still, his stomach ached, and when he stood in the kitchen and put the first bite in his mouth with a fork he found in the drying rack, it tasted a little better than barf. Not much better, but a little. He ate the whole thing standing up and then he looked around for the dishwasher, because that's where dirty dishes go, but didn't find one. Then he remembered Aunt Jo washing her plate by hand and he saw the dish soap and the rag but he didn't want to start washing it because then Aunt Jo would hear him from the living room and know what he was doing.

He stood there for a while holding his dirty plate. Nothing went through his head, except that he was standing in a different city than he'd been standing in that morning. Besides that, everything inside was blank. Finally he gave up and washed the dish, only he squirted out too much soap so he ended up filling the entire sink with suds.

"How about dessert?" Aunt Jo said from the archway. He froze. Maybe if he stood really still and didn't breathe, then he wouldn't really be here standing in an ugly yellow kitchen with a stranger asking him grape-soda questions like *How about dessert?*

"No thanks."

"You like chocolate? I've got half a chocolate pie in the fridge."

That was a trick question because she knew he liked chocolate ever since the time she'd come to visit on his fifth birthday and he'd snuck away to the kitchen and eaten half the chocolate cake and everyone had caught him sitting on the cake plate covered in frosting.

"I like vanilla."

Aunt Jo frowned. She looked like a picture of an angry,

leather-faced turtle Sam had seen once in a library book.

"Okay, well, it'll be there if you want some."

"I won't."

Aunt Jo didn't say anything. Sam could feel her looking at him, and he waited for her to get angry or say that she was disappointed in his attitude or make some other grape-soda move, but she didn't. She just stood there and he stood there, and he felt kind of like Jimmy Erickson, who was this blue jay from school who once made the lunch lady cry, but so what?

(Pa said *blue jay* whenever he really wanted to say *jerk*, since blue jays are the jerks of the bird world and they spend all day making other birds miserable.)

"How about I show you to your room?"

Sam shrugged like he didn't care either way, but really he was ready to go to sleep. He grabbed his backpack from the hall and his suitcase and the De Havilland Mosquito bomber and followed Aunt Jo upstairs. Her metal leg moved almost as smoothly as her right, and Sam had to take the steps two at a time to keep up.

"This is my room here, and you're this way at the end of the hall." Sam took a quick look inside Aunt Jo's room and saw a single wooden chair with a pile of neatly folded clothes on the edge of a bed. The bed looked hard, like maybe she had a block of wood underneath instead of a mattress.

His room was all the way at the other end, which was fine by him.

"You've got extra sheets in the closet and towels. Your bathroom's through here so we don't have to share, but I do expect you to keep it clean."

He looked around at everything but didn't really look because he didn't want to do it in front of Aunt Jo and, besides, he didn't plan on staying.

"There's a new toothbrush and toothpaste in the bathroom, soap too." She waited. He didn't want to look at her face, so he looked at her shoes instead, white orthopedics, and at her pants, the left leg billowing out around her metal ankle, and at her fingers that kept tugging on the poker chip she wore around her neck. He wanted her to leave, but she didn't.

She came in close like maybe she was going to hug him, only he took a step back and hit the edge of the bathroom door instead.

"Sorry," she said as the door rattled. She reached for him, but then she didn't and her hands went back to tugging on her necklace. "Well, I'll let you get unpacked."

He nodded because maybe that would make her go away. Aunt Jo went to stand in the doorway but didn't leave. "If you need anything, I'm right down the hall."

Nod.

"Good night, Sam. I'm glad you're here."

Nod.

"If you need anything . . ."

He stood still, neck throbbing from looking down at his shoes, and finally he heard the door click. He let his bags slump off his shoulders and drop to the floor.

4

MAYBE IT WAS ONLY EIGHT o'clock and maybe he didn't want to lie down in the grape-soda bed with the scratchy green blanket, but he did it anyway. He didn't unpack or open the brand-new toothbrush or take off his shoes. He did turn off the lights and open the puke-green curtains so he could look out at the ugly Oklahoma sky.

The bed was hard, like maybe *all* the beds in this house were made of wood instead of foam or feathers or whatever mattresses were usually made of. He closed his eyes. Maybe he fell asleep, because he woke up to someone scratching on the window. A long shadow stretched across the floor, lit from behind by moonlight. It must have been the moon, but it shone so bright it reminded him of headlights. The shadow reached up and dragged long fingernails down the glass.

It was like that time when he was little and he'd woken up with one foot in the swamp because he'd been sleep-walking, only he didn't know that yet and he couldn't figure out where he was or how he'd gotten so wet. He sat up and his clothes were one big pool of sweat, and the shadow kept beating at the window with this slow, steady beat and then the screech of sharp nails.

He shook his head to see if he was dreaming, and then he wondered if maybe he'd walked all the way to the neighbors' house in his sleep, but that was impossible since the closest neighbors were all the way across the swamp. He slid off the bed, which was hard as wood, and realized he was still wearing his shoes.

The room swam into focus around him. He saw the suitcase, the backpack, the De Havilland bomber with a broken propeller. And then he saw the shadow man clawing at his window to be let in. Except then the shadow wobbled and shrank, and it didn't look like a man anymore but a cat.

Shivering a little thanks to the sweat dripping down his back, he opened the window. The metal shrieked. He stepped back as the cat leaped from the windowsill to the bed in a single bound. It was the same cat with the smashed-in face. The one Sam could swear he'd seen before, only how could he have? A cat with half a face wasn't exactly easy to forget.

Without stopping to acknowledge Sam's presence, the cat scratched at Sam's pillow like he owned the place, fluffing it into a puffy nest and then settling down with his head tucked into his belly. He blinked and studied Sam with his glowing silver eye.

Sam stared back, and then the cat covered his face with

his tail, as if to say *enough with the staring already*, and soon he was snoring. Partly Sam was thinking who did that cat think he was sneaking into his room in the middle of the night and stealing his pillow? Partly he was glad for the company, because he remembered now that this wasn't his room or his house or even his state, and a creepy cat was better company than no one at all.

He looked around the room and saw a clock that he hadn't noticed the night before. It sat on top of a red dresser and was shaped like a plane with a clock dial for a propeller. 5:27 a.m. Sam looked around to see all the things he hadn't bothered to notice the night before because he hadn't wanted to see them: the red dresser right across from the wood-block bed with a different fish painted on every drawer, that clock shaped like a World War II biplane, cowboy wallpaper with the same Wild West saloons and gunslingers on horseback repeated every few feet, a rope hung up on the wall with nails like it was about to lasso one of the wallpaper horses, a nightstand on either side of the bed, one with the same crusty yellow lamp as downstairs, one with three photographs in tiny silver frames.

Sam walked over to the other side of the bed, his shoes creaking on the floorboards. He sank down on the mattress, opposite the cat, and that wrinkly old gutter rat kept right on snoozing. One by one he picked up the photographs and examined the black-and-white images. The first showed a girl in overalls towering over a runty boy with a mischievous smile. He was holding up a line full of fish, and she was scowling down at him with her arms crossed over her chest. Even a stranger could pick out Pa, with his smile that tilted more to the right than the left and that sparkle in his eyes that said he was fixing to get into a whole heap of trouble. Aunt Jo looked like a giant next to Pa, even though she was supposed to be the baby sister, and her expression was just as sour and cold-hearted as ever.

The second was a photo of Pops, except he had dark hair combed down tight around his ears instead of a puffy white cloud and he had his arm around the biggest hog Sam had ever seen. The hog had a medal around its neck and Pops was smiling like he'd just won the lotto, so it must have been from some old state fair.

Sam set the frame down carefully and then picked up the third. His stomach seized before he even had a chance to look close. A single gray eye stared up at him, though he was pretty sure it would have shone silver had the photo been in color. It was another picture of Pa as a boy, but in this one he was all alone except for the mangy ball of fur spilling from his arms.

"Mother, Mary, and Joseph," Sam said, which wasn't just Aunt Jo's favorite way of expressing surprise, but Pa's too.

He looked over at the cat snoozing in his spot and then back at the cat in the photo. True, the moon wasn't too bright and he hadn't bothered to turn on a light, but how many cats could there be with only half a face? How many cats with the exact same puckered skin and a nose that looked half normal and half like mashed-in Play-Doh?

Sam stood up, still gripping the frame like maybe that cat was some kind of feline vampire with a secret plan to suck his blood. The cat didn't wake up, though, no matter how long Sam stood there, and so he went and sat in the windowsill where he could keep an eye on him. His heartbeat calmed down as the cat's snoring got louder. He didn't know much about vampires, but probably they didn't snore.

Still keeping an eye out, he undid the little fasteners on the back of the frame and slid out the photo. From his new spot, the light was bright enough to make out details he hadn't noticed before, like the fact that Pa was flashing his signature grin, the one he always made just before, or after, getting into trouble. Sam could also see that he was standing in front of a tree.

Sam thought it might be a maple tree since the leaves had three big blades at the top and two tiny ones at the bottom. The cat's fuzzy tail wrapped around Pa's back, and that was when Sam saw the hole gouged out of the center of the tree, looking just like an old, crinkly mouth. Sam held the photo closer, so it was nearly touching the tip of his nose. He traced each one of the branches with his eyes, taking in every crook and jag and, even though he couldn't be sure, he thought it was the same tree where he'd first met the cat.

He turned the photo over and there, scrawled in Pa's messy script, were the words, "One-Eye, summer of 1983."

But how could he still be alive almost forty years later? Sam looked from the words to the cat, and he got the same feeling he had whenever Pa started telling one of his stories. Like the world was about to stop, and as soon as Pa started talking, he'd be transported someplace where all the boring rules of this world didn't apply. His neck went tingly and he could almost taste the bittersweet smell of Pa's chewing tobacco and hear the crisp pop as he opened a warm can of Orange Crush.

Sam closed his eyes, lost in memories of Pa, when two things happened all at once. The door to his room swung open, and One-Eye woke with a snarl, leaping out the second-story window. Sam didn't know where to look first. He didn't hear One-Eye land, but he did hear the doorknob bang against the wall and crunch into the plaster.

He stood up fast, hitting his head on the open window and then grabbing his forehead to rub away the black dots invading his vision. The photo fell from his hands and he readied himself to fight, but then Aunt Jo stepped into a slant of moonlight.

She was wearing a green flannel nightgown, and her eyes were big, like a little kid who'd just woken up from a nightmare. But that wasn't what caught Sam's attention. She was using short metal crutches to stay upright, and there was only one leg sticking out the bottom of her gown. He tried his best not to stare at the space where her other leg should have been, but it was hard to look away.

"Are you okay? I thought I heard something before," she said, blinking the sleep from her eyes.

"Don't worry," he said. "It was just some old cat."

She came over to look out the window, frowning. "In the house?"

"Yup." He trained his eyes on the ceiling, the wall, trying to look anywhere but at the leg.

"How'd it get in?"

Sam shrugged. "I opened the window."

They stood all quiet for a minute, except that Sam's heart was pounding about a million miles an hour in his chest. It was all so creepy and awkward, and how had that cat found him all the way up here anyway? They both looked out at the lawn with the square bushes and the white picket fence, but no cat.

"Sorry, I guess I was having a nightmare. For a minute, I forgot there was someone else in the house." Aunt Jo followed his gaze down to her missing leg. Dang, he'd been staring again. She didn't say anything, and he breathed a sigh of relief.

"Yeah, must've been a nightmare," Sam said, but what he really wanted to say was that he wished she would forget about him so he could get out of this stuffy house and go back home. Where strangers didn't break into his room in the middle of the night and, oh yeah, where he didn't have to worry about visitations from weird, possibly dead cats.

"Well, now that we're both up, how about pancakes? I make a mean chocolate-chip-peanut-butter batter. Your pa used to say it should win an award."

Sam looked at the clock and the glowing propeller hands. It was 5:42 in the morning.

Aunt Jo must have noticed where he was looking, because her dried lips split into a smile. "That's one thing you'll learn about me. I'm an early riser. Why wait for the sun when there's stuff to get done? You know what I mean?"

"Not really."

"'Rise and shine sleepy time,' that's my motto." She looked Sam up and down, and the weight of her gaze made his skin itch. Why couldn't she just leave him alone? "You look like you could use some pancakes. Wash your hands and follow me."

He didn't move an inch as she retreated down the hallway. His first thought was *Who the heck eats pancakes at 5:42 in the morning?* followed quickly by *Who the heck did this lady think she was telling him to wash his hands?* Pa hardly ever washed his hands, except when he got back from fishing and sometimes not even then. Was she saying that he was dirty, or that his pa was dirty? What made her so great and fancy? Just because she lived in an ugly old dollhouse with yellow plates in the middle of some creepy ghost town.

Sam went downstairs, but he didn't wash his hands. He decided to think more on the ghost cat later, if that's really what it was, when his brain wasn't a huge bowl of mush.

By the time he sat down at the kitchen table, Aunt Jo had already whipped up the batter and was spooning it into a hot frying pan. He noticed that she was wearing her artificial leg again, a pair of stiff khakis riding high over her white orthopedic shoes. His chair squeaked when he pulled it out and then again when he sat down. He told himself that he wasn't going to eat any pancakes because it was too early and no way they'd be as good as Pa's. Pa made his pancakes with blueberries and cinnamon and his secret ingredient, beer. All the beer cooked off in the pan, so it wasn't like you got drunk or anything, but they were still better than whatever Aunt Jo was about to make.

But then, when she heaped three fat pancakes on his plate and covered them in steamy maple syrup, he had to admit that they didn't smell as terrible as he'd expected. Besides, Pa would probably tell him to be polite and eat up, since Aunt Jo was his baby sister, even if she had disappeared for the past four years and probably didn't care whether Sam lived or died. Not really.

Sam ate his pancakes.

"Now, I'll do the dishes this morning," Aunt Jo said,

standing up from the table with a grunt. "But starting tonight, that'll be your job. School bus comes at seven-thirty sharp, so you'd better go upstairs and unpack. And I expect you to take a shower every day you're in this house. I may not have any kids, but I know boys, and let me tell you, when he was your age your pa could clear out a room quicker than a hog on an all-burrito diet. We'll have none of that stink in my house."

If Aunt Jo had sprouted horns and turned into a green, blobby slime demon, Sam wouldn't have been more surprised than he was right then. Any lingering thoughts about ghost cats and mysterious trees got zapped clean out of his head. What did she mean about school? He'd just gotten here. He'd barely even slept, and now he was supposed to get on a bus full of strangers in the wrong state with a belly full of the wrong pancakes and pretend like everything was normal? Who did this lady think she was? Not his pa, that's for sure, and where did she get off saying Pa stank?

He stood up like a zombie and said nothing, because the words were zooming around so fast and sharp in his head he couldn't catch hold of just one.

"You can have the first hot water," she said, as if it was the nicest thing anyone had ever done for him. "But don't use it all up. Some people need coffee to get going. Me, all I need is a big plate of pancakes and a nice hot shower."

She looked at him like she was expecting him to answer,

which was a total grape-soda move since she hadn't even asked a question.

"Well, don't just stand there. Time's a ticking. Towels are in the closet where I showed you."

Sam didn't have to be told twice. He headed upstairs and he only tripped once, on the top step, which was okay since by then Aunt Jo couldn't see him. He closed the door to his room harder than he intended and then sat down on the floor and stared at his shoes. They were covered in dirt, and he could tell it was Oklahoma dirt because it looked red instead of brown like normal.

He sniffed under his armpit. Maybe he did stink, a little, but he knew one thing for certain: no way he was stepping foot in that shower unless maybe it was to turn on the hot water and let it all run out before Aunt Jo had a chance to use it. True, that was some serious blue-jay thinking, but the way he saw it, he was just acting in self-defense since he hadn't asked to be kidnapped and dragged halfway across the country. He sat there for a while thinking of what he'd say if Aunt Jo came upstairs and asked why he wasn't in the shower. Then he looked at the clock that said it was 7:08 a.m., which had to be a mistake, because the last time he'd checked it was 5:47.

"Better get dressed!" Aunt Jo called from downstairs. He waited, but she didn't make any mention of the shower.

A gust of wind rattled through the open window, like

50

maybe it knew just what he was thinking, and what he was thinking was that he had to escape. He slid his backpack full of clothes onto his shoulders and then changed his mind and dumped out a bunch of socks and underwear and shoved the De Havilland bomber in there instead. He raised up the window as high as it would go, trying not to squeak, but it did squeak, and it wouldn't even go as high as he wanted.

He swung one leg over and bent forward so he could stick out his head. He looked down at the patchy grass and up at the leaves of the giant maple, bathed in sunlight. It would have been nice, lucky even, if the branches had been close enough to reach or if Aunt Jo had an awning or even a gutter he could use to break his fall.

Too bad his luck had run out.

Instead, it was a straight drop. Sam swung his other leg over so now he was sitting in the windowsill with just his butt and both hands to steady him. If he jumped, he would probably break a leg, which he imagined would feel a lot better than the time Pa got his foot run over by that lawn mower, but not by much. The wind picked up, like maybe it wanted him to fall. It lifted him just enough so he got a good sense of what falling might feel like, and then he scrambled back inside and shut the window, not even worrying about the shriek.

Footsteps pounded up the stairs, and Aunt Jo threw open

the door like she owned the place, and maybe she did, but still. She looked at his backpack and his clothes, which were the same ones he'd slept in the night before. He expected her to say something about a shower, but instead she pulled him into a hug so tight it made his ribs hurt.

He had to admit that Aunt Jo smelled better than before, like soap, and flowery shampoo, and now that she'd decided to invade his personal space without asking maybe it was true that his underwear was starting to feel a little crusty, but still. Still. Who said he wanted a grape-soda hug?

"I know it's hard," she said, crushing his ribs, "but it'll get easier. And the good thing is that we can get through it together."

He stood still and didn't struggle, even though it was a miracle he didn't suffocate. Finally, she let him go, and his ribs expanded again inside his chest.

"Maybe you should stay home from school today, and I can help you unpack. That way we'll have a chance to catch up." She tried on a fake smile, but it crumpled. "I know . . . well . . . I know I haven't been around the past few years, not like I wanted to be, but I'm here now. What do you say?"

"No, thanks. I'd rather go to school."

"Okay, if you're sure."

"I'm sure." He stared down at the wooden floor, which was ugly and rough instead of smooth and polished. Maybe he was being kind of a blue jay, but who could blame him? Who?

"Got everything you need?"

He didn't answer. Another blue-jay move, but those pancakes had started to work their way up the back of his throat. It was barf-bag time all over again.

"Bus'll be here any minute."

"Okay."

He waited for her to say something else, like maybe where the bus stop was or even what the school was called, which she'd failed to mention the day before, but she just stood there and he just stood there, and then he heard the unmistakable whoosh of air brakes that meant the bus had just pulled to a stop outside.

"Bye, I guess."

Maybe Aunt Jo finally said something, but he didn't wait to find out. He ran down the stairs and through the hall and straight out the door. Even though the wind was dry and it stung his cheeks, a weight lifted off him the second he went outside.

He climbed onto the bus and slid into the seat right behind the driver. Nobody liked to sit right behind the driver, at least back home, so he figured this way everybody would leave him alone. They did. Except that he could still hear them talking. He dug around in his backpack, which was full of clothes and comics and half of everything he owned, not to mention the De Havilland Mosquito bomber.

His hoodie was wrapped around a jar of gator teeth that he and Pa had collected on the shore by their house, and he unraveled it and pulled it on, lowering the hood. At the very bottom of the bag, next to his field guide to Louisiana snakes, he found his earbuds tangled in a knot as big as his fist. Of course. It took three more stops before he finally freed up the wires. Once, a girl with faded purple hair almost sat down next to him, but he didn't move his bag off the seat and she kept walking. That whole time he had to listen to people jabber about stuff that didn't matter, like whether or not some kid named Ray had peed his pants and what some grape-soda YouTuber had eaten for breakfast and why the cafeteria had to serve Frito pie every Thursday even though everyone agreed it looked like barf.

Barf again. Great.

Finally, the wires came loose and he stuffed the earbuds in so hard he maybe burst an eardrum. Almost. Listening to music made everything better, because he could pretend that he wasn't surrounded by blue jays and he didn't even mind that the bus ride took a hundred years since maybe there was only one bus in the whole grape-soda town.

He looked out the window some, but everything was dry and dusty and boring, even the farm equipment and the fields of dead grass and sad-eyed cows. It turned out that Aunt Jo lived in the nicest part of town, and most other people lived in trailers or houses with droopy roofs or houses with dirty bedsheets draped like curtains around the front porch.

After a while, Sam got so used to the twang of the music, Clifton Chenier and His Red Hot Louisiana Band, and the hum of the window vibrating against his cheek, that he almost fell asleep, but then the bus started up a hill, and at the top of that hill Sam saw a tree.

Glass crunched under the bus's tires, but it kept right on going, moving slow and steady, which gave Sam a chance to get a good, long look. It was a maple all right, because now he could see the dead leaves lying in broken pieces on the ground, and they had three points on top and two on the bottom. A sliver of sun peeked over the horizon and, in the orangey-gold light, he saw strange sparkles suddenly appear, dotting the patchy grass and the peeling bark, especially near the hollow.

Sam leaned closer, pressing his forehead against the glass. The hollow wasn't only shimmering, it was moving. Maybe it was a trick of the light, but he swore he saw a writhing mass of something gathered around the opening, like a swarm of bees spilling out of that creepy, shriveled mouth. The bus bounced up to the top of the hill, where Sam had the best view.

Suddenly, he saw that it wasn't bees spilling out of the hole but dragonflies, shimmering greens and iridescent blues, their translucent wings breaking up the sunlight so the entire blob of bodies seemed to twinkle.

The bus crested the hill and bumped on past, but Sam could still spot dragonflies resting here and there on the grass, like tiny shards of blue-and-green glass.

5

THE SCHOOL WAS CALLED HOLLER Junior High—so original—and it was a big gray building with three wings, the biggest one for the elementary and the other two for the junior high and high school. There were no headphones allowed in Holler Junior High, as some guy with an ugly white mustache informed him, so he shoved the earbuds down into the bottom of his backpack and stood in the office like a total blue jay waiting for someone to notice him.

"Let me guess," said the ugly mustache guy, who'd been watching him stand there like a blue jay for a while. "Samuel West. I have to say, son, we weren't expecting you so soon, but I like your initiative. You're a real self-starter, I take it. Tell me, when'd you get into town?"

Sam wanted to ask the guy why he was being such a stalker and if he could maybe get his crusty old mustache out of his face, but instead he looked down at his shoes and said, "Last night."

The guy whistled, which made him look like the world's biggest can of grape soda, because of the way his mustache flapped on the air like wings. "I knew your pa," the old guy said, and then maybe he saw the disbelieving look on Sam's face, because he laughed, the kind of laugh that's mostly spit, and Sam was glad he still had on his hood because it blocked out the worst of it. "That's right. Had your pa in class my first year teaching and wowee, that boy put me through the wringer. Did he ever tell you about the time he let a possum in the teacher's lounge? Cutest thing you ever seen, until it started snapping."

Sam didn't know what to say to that, mostly because he was still stuck on the fact that Pa had gone to this same school.

"Name's Mr. Redding." He offered his old-guy hand, and Sam had no choice but to shake it. It was cold and wrinkly, like raw chicken. "Follow me, son, and I'll get you sorted out. Goodness gracious, you sure don't pack light. What've you got in that thing anyway?" He lifted the flap of Sam's backpack and peeked inside. "Looks like a De Havilland bomber circa World War II? I see you know your planes, Mr. West."

Sam didn't say anything, since surely touching a stranger's backpack was against some kind of school rule, and what did Mr. Redding know about anything anyway, apart from growing the world's ugliest mustache?

"Well, on we go." They went through a grape-soda door down a grape-soda hallway with linoleum tile that you could tell was supposed to be white but was really yellow. His locker was right across from a trophy case with a lot of dusty trophies and team pictures inside. The really annoying part was that the lockers didn't have locks, even though lock was part of the name.

"Don't worry. We run on the honor system around here, but you can bring your own lock tomorrow if you want." He placed his old-guy hand on Sam's shoulder. "How're you holding up, son? Your auntie told me what happened. Terrible, just terrible, but it must be a comfort now being back with family."

It took Sam a while to realize that by family he meant Aunt Jo. He stood there for about a hundred years thinking how he'd like to punch Mr. Redding in the face, and Mr. Redding stood there looking like maybe he was gonna cry, which was pure grape soda, and also a lie, because he didn't really know Pa and even if he did he should know enough to keep his grape-soda mouth shut.

Finally the bell rang. Sam shoved his backpack in the locker, not even bothering to take out a pencil since he hadn't thought to bring one, and headed down the hall. The problem was he didn't know where he was going, and so Mr. Redding had to run after him, and by the time he caught up he was breathing like the engine on Pa's '68 Pontiac Sunbird. The same Sunbird Aunt Jo had let some guy cart off to the junkyard, never mind all the years he and Pa had spent getting her to run again. The same Sunbird that had veered off the road the night Pa . . . the night he . . .

"You can't get rid of me that easily, Mr. West. Classroom's this way."

Great.

The class turned out to be the room right next to the trophy case. The girl with purple hair from the bus was standing in the doorway smirking at him, and he wanted to tell her that it was rude to stare, especially when your head looked like a dried-up eggplant, but instead he kept his words to himself.

It turned out they did school different in middle-of-nowhere Oklahoma, because there was only one teacher for all of seventh grade, and he was the guy with a mustache like a toilet brush. There were maybe twelve kids in the whole class, which meant there were plenty of extra desks, and so Sam took a seat at the very back by the window.

Everybody else was sitting in the front two rows, but Mr. Redding didn't ask him to move up, so maybe he wasn't all bad. During the morning announcements, Sam looked around at everybody else with their textbooks and binders and their little plastic boxes filled with pencils. He tried to remember what he'd done with his binder and the red canvas bag where he kept his pencils, but all that seemed like something from another Sam, one who didn't exist anymore. Probably all his school stuff was rotting at the bottom of a dumpster with a bunch of dirty tinsel and Pa's Big Mouth Bass.

Once the announcements were over, Mr. Redding asked if Sam wanted to introduce himself.

"No thanks."

The girl with purple hair laughed, but Mr. Redding pretended not to notice. "Class, it gives me great pleasure to introduce Mr. Samuel West. He comes to us all the way from Louisiana. Let's give him a warm Wildcats welcome."

His words were followed by this long silence broken by a smattering of applause. Sam kept his eyes pinned to his desk, except he couldn't help looking up at the purple-haired girl. She was smiling at him the way you'd smile at some loser you felt sorry for, except he could tell she wasn't really sorry.

Sam looked out the window for the rest of the day. Usually, he would daydream about flying bombers in World War II or wrestling gators or finally beating Andy Hamlin at the hundred-yard dash, but today his brain was a blob. A big gray blob that clogged up his ears and oozed out the edges of his eyeballs. Except it didn't really, because if it did he'd probably be dead.

Nothing interesting happened at all until right after Mr. Redding switched from history to science. Sam was looking out the window, minding his own business, when a long shadow stretched across the grass, coming from behind

61

a row of scraggly bushes. He searched for the source of the shadow, the taffy arms and legs and the rib cage so thin you could pick out each and every bone. Then the shadow wobbled and collapsed, and a twisted gray shape slinked out from behind the nearest bush, blinking at him with a single silver eye.

Despite all of Pa's stories about fairy folk and swamp goblins and things that went bump in the night, Sam had always considered himself a realist. Stories were stories, and no matter how good a story was, that didn't make it a fact. But, realist or not, that cat gave him the creeps. Sure, maybe it wasn't really a ghost cat, because that was impossible. Totally. Not. Possible. And maybe that shadow was a normal shadow and not some weird shape-shifting shadow that was following him around town like a . . . crap . . . like a ghost. He swallowed, trying to work some moisture back into his mouth.

"Mr. West, please join the other students at the board."

Mr. Redding's voice drew Sam back to the classroom and he blinked in confusion at the sea of empty desks. It took him a minute to realize that everyone else was standing at the long whiteboard on the front wall, furiously writing words like: *cows*, *cars*, and *factories*.

Sam got up, only he must have gotten up too fast, because for a second his vision went spotty. He looked back outside near the ring of bushes and the green metal garbage can and the rusty bench, but the cat and his creepy silver eye had gone.

"We're listing sources of greenhouse gases," Mr. Redding was saying, but Sam wasn't really listening because just then a dragonfly landed on the window, followed by another and another. Each of the dragonflies landed with a dull thud, followed by the twitter of buzzing wings. One by one, the other students turned to watch, staring as the growing mass of dragonflies slowly blocked out the sun.

"Class, let's focus on our work," Mr. Redding said, but even he didn't seem convinced. The whole time, Sam kept thinking about what Aunt Jo had said. That it was too dry in Holler for dragonflies. Then why were they here? Because one thing was certain: they were a long way from water.

At lunch Sam lined up like everybody else. He still had twenty dollars in his pocket that Pa had given him for cleaning bird poop off the Sunbird. Too bad the Sunbird was trash now and so all that time he'd spent scraping off poop with a toothbrush had been for nothing. At his old school you got to pick your food, but here a lady with her hair in a shower cap scooped the same chili on top of everybody's Fritos, and he had to admit, it really did look like barf.

When he got to the front of the line and it was time for him to hand the twenty to a different lady with hot pink nails and matching lipstick, he just stood there clenching the bill in his fist. He remembered the day Pa had given it to him like it was happening right now. He could smell Pa's chewing tobacco and oily jeans, and he could see his crooked smile and his missing teeth and the motor grease under his nails, exactly like Pa was standing right there in front of him and not suffocating in some box six feet underground.

He stuffed the twenty back in his pocket and left the tray with the barfy chili sitting on the counter. Some people called after him, but he didn't pay attention and instead went through the first door he found. It led into a courtyard. A short stone wall ran along the edges, holding back these huge bushes with white flowers that didn't look too ugly if you squinted. Sam took a seat on the wall in a shady spot where no one else was sitting.

Good.

Great.

He was alone.

Except being alone meant that he started to think, and his thoughts were like spiders that hid away in cracks anytime you tried to swat them. But you really did want to swat them, because they were big nasty spiders, but it was even easier to pretend like they didn't exist. And the thoughts he was scared of thinking had nothing to do with ghost cats or shape-shifting shadows, but they had everything to do with Pa and Holler and how sometimes he wished he were dead too because at least then he wouldn't be alone.

To get his mind off things, he watched all the people coming and going, but the problem was that they weren't really all that interesting. Part of him wished he'd taken the Frito pie, because at least then he'd have a distraction even if it did taste like barf.

"Hi."

He looked up and realized that he'd been so busy trying to distract himself that he hadn't noticed the purple-haired girl standing over him staring with her huge, buggy sunglasses.

"Hey."

She sat down next to him.

"You've got something in your hair," she said, which he figured was probably some kind of trick. "Seriously, there's a huge bug on your head. Can't you feel that?"

Sam swatted at his hair, and sure enough, his hand touched something solid. The big green thing dropped to the grass, and then its motor started up and it buzzed away.

"That's the first time I've ever seen a dragonfly around here." She adjusted her giant sunglasses before peering up into the sky, probably searching for the dragonfly's shimmer.

"I guess you must not look around very much."

"Do you know the last time it rained in Holler?" she said, like maybe she hadn't heard him.

"No, do you?"

"April fifth of last year. I remember because I was outside testing Percy."

"Who's Percy? Your dog?"

"That's the name of my first glider. But it's broken now."

"Oh."

"I'm building a new one."

The girl didn't say anything for a while, but just kept staring at the sky with her ginormous sunglasses that were the same pale purple as her hair. "My dad used to say that dragonflies were bad luck, since they only come around when it rains."

Sam looked at the girl a little closer. She hid her hands in the sleeves of her oversize flannel. "I think your dad was right," Sam said.

"Not me. Personally, I always liked the rain."

"Oh." Sam considered. "You said 'used to say.' Does that mean he's not around anymore?"

She shrugged, but turned back to face him. Her glasses were so dark that he couldn't see anything but his own reflection looking all stretched out and wavy in the curved plastic. "He's around somewhere, just not in Holler. It's me and Mom now."

"Oh."

The girl turned her eyes back to the sky, still searching for dragonflies. He wanted to know what had happened to her dad, but couldn't figure out how to ask the question.

"I heard your dad died," she said, without taking her eyes off the clouds.

Maybe that was how you asked the question. He wanted to be angry at her for saying it out loud, but he wasn't. "Yeah, I guess he did."

"I'm sorry."

They didn't talk anymore after that, but the weird thing was, it felt okay. She sat there, and Sam sat there, and somehow his thoughts weren't so much like spiders anymore but like normal, everyday thoughts.

A bell rang.

The rest of the day wasn't so bad, and he kept sneaking glances at the girl with purple hair, but not because he liked her or anything. When school was over, he sat down on this brick wall out front to wait for Aunt Jo, and the girl sat down next to him.

"So, how was your first day?" she said, and she was wearing her giant sunglasses again, and now that he thought about it, they made her look more like a movie star than a bug.

"Not completely terrible."

"I guess that's okay, then."

"Yup."

He racked his brain, trying to think of more words, but he couldn't. And the girl shifted in her seat, and he realized that he didn't even know her name, and he was going to ask her, but that was when he saw it. Some kid being loud over by the flagpole, getting ready to launch a plane that looked an awful lot like the De Havilland Mosquito bomber. He shot up, and when he got closer he saw his backpack and all of his other stuff spread out on the grass like somebody had dumped it there, including his underwear and his pictures of Pa and the jar full of gator teeth that had hit a rock and shattered. He'd totally forgotten about his backpack sitting in the pointless locker that didn't even have a lock.

"Hey!" he shouted, and a bunch of the kids who were picking through his stuff looked up, but he made a bee-line for the jerk launching his plane, only he was too late. The kid swung back his arm, really swung it back, and Sam didn't even see what he looked like, only his ugly red T-shirt, before he slammed him to the ground and started punching.

He didn't hear the plane crack into the wall or feel Mr. Redding pull him off, but the next thing he knew, he tasted blood in his mouth and Mr. Redding had him wrapped up in his wrinkly old-guy hands. A bunch of teachers swooped in and shooed everyone away, except for the jerk who was busy spitting out a tooth.

"You'd better come with me, Mr. West." Mr. Redding loosened his grip, and that was all the time Sam needed. He bolted.

"Wait!" someone said, and he actually turned back around, because it was the girl. She was picking up the plane and she started to walk toward him, but he didn't wait. He snatched it from her hands without so much as a thank you.

"Mr. West!"

He ignored Mr. Redding and took off, leaving his underwear and his pictures and everything else he owned behind. The hot wind cut into his skin. He rounded the side of the ugly gray building, bolting up the hill and over the dead grass, the pieces of his plane clutched so tight he couldn't feel his fingers. He was just running and not caring where he was going, and after a while he stopped and flung the plane as hard as he could. It split into three pieces in the air, and then this gray shadow hurtled out of nowhere and attacked the biggest piece. Both the plane and the shadow hit the dirt and rolled, and when they finally settled down again, there was One-Eye with a propeller blade clutched in his mouth.

His silver eye flashed, lips curling back in a grin, and then he turned and sprinted away.

"Get back here!" Sam screamed. He ran, even though the plane was already broken and so who cared, but also he cared, but the cat was running too fast and then he leaped into the air and the next thing Sam knew One-Eye had disappeared inside the hollow of that creepy old tree.

Gone.

Just like that.

Sam froze, his face inches from the hole, and a shiver prickled like needles up his back as he saw that the tree wasn't covered in bark anymore, but a thick blanket of shimmery blue and green bodies, hundreds, maybe thousands of them, all shifting and flashing their veiny, translucent wings.

He stopped breathing and reached his hand into the hole. His fingers didn't touch fur or the rough bark at the back of the tree; they kept going. He reached in farther, even though now the dragonfly wings were brushing his cheek, and he touched wet grass and leaves and something long and spidery that felt an awful lot like Spanish moss.

He pulled his hand back, and moisture glistened on his fingertips. A warm breeze issued from inside the hole, thawing out his icy skin. It smelled like home.

As if on cue, the dragonflies began to peel away from the bark, pouring like an iridescent blue-green wave back into the hollow. Once the last dragonfly had disappeared, Sam allowed himself one final deep breath before climbing headfirst into the gaping, shadowy mouth.

IN THE DARKNESS, SAM GOT that feeling again like he was teetering on the edge of a cliff. He drew in a deep breath, leaned forward—and then he was falling. As he plummeted, dragonflies flitted past in the dark passageway, the frantic beat of their wings tickling his face. Salty sweat stung his eyes, bark scraped his cheeks and, before he knew what was happening, he'd dropped face-first onto a bed of thick leaves. He blinked, head still spinning, and noticed that the leaves were the size of hubcaps, all moist with dew. He found the propeller blade from the De Havilland sitting in a patch of grass and slid it in his pocket. A curtain of Spanish moss brushed his cheek as he turned over to stare into the canopy of a dense forest.

It looked familiar somehow, but everything was larger and brighter and the light streaming through in glittering slants seemed strangely solid, almost like he could reach out and touch it.

He rolled over and came face-to-face with a bullfrog snoozing in a pool of muddy water, except it wasn't a normal bullfrog. This one was at least as big as a small dog, and it fixed Sam with an irritated glare before hopping away and splattering his shirt with water. All around, the trees and grass and reeds grew twice as tall as normal, and everything was dripping sparkling water droplets, as if he'd arrived at the tail end of a rainstorm. The air smelled rainy, too, and it hung heavy against his skin just like the humid air back home.

Sam sat up and searched the trees for any sign of One-Eye. His whole body tingled head to toe, but whatever questions he had got shut out by the surge of excitement bubbling in his gut. This place didn't just look familiar. These trees might be huge, but they were tupelo trees, just like in Bayou St. George, and over there through the tall grass, he could see the green, glassy surface of a swamp. His swamp.

At least, he thought it was. It had to be.

He ran toward Ol' Tired Eyes, crashing through the grass that grew up past his shoulders, moving with such speed that he took a few steps in the water before realizing he'd gone too far.

"Can't be," he said out loud, and he didn't even care that there was nobody around to listen, because here it was. There, on the other side of the swamp, sat a tiny white house on stilts with a wooden dock built out over the water, and that wasn't huge or strange, but normal size. Just the way he remembered. And, if he squinted, he could see a can of Orange Crush sitting on the edge of that dock, just where he'd left it, and once he'd settled down long enough to listen, he heard Pa's beer-can wind chimes clinking and clanking on the breeze, and it sounded even more beautiful than ever.

That tingling coming from deep under his skin grew until his whole body was vibrating, like he had a hundred dragonflies motoring away inside his stomach. He took another step into the water, and another, and he might have swum the whole way, gators or no gators, if he hadn't noticed Pa's canoe bobbing in the reeds a few feet to his right. It was tied to a stick buried deep in the mud. Sam was reaching over to untether it when a hand clamped down on his shoulder.

He spun around, half expecting to find a long, thin shadow towering over him. What he found instead was a boy.

"There you are. I must say, it took you long enough." Sunlight sizzled in the boy's eyes, the color of fresh straw, and he fixed Sam with a familiar crooked grin. "I was beginning to think you'd forgotten what time it was." The boy showed off his watch, a Hamilton Aviation watch circa 1942. "Better head over while you still can. The doorway won't stay open long."

He sucked on a blade of grass, drawing it through the gap in his bottom teeth. That was the same gap Pa had gotten from sparring with Bobby Joe's pet raccoon as a toddler. Sam didn't move or breathe. Heck, he didn't even sweat.

"You're him." Sam couldn't believe what he was saying, but it was true. The Boy looked exactly like Pa from the old pictures in his room, back when he was Sam's age. "Pa? Is that really you?" Words pounded in Sam's head, but none of them did justice to the chaos raging in his brain.

The Boy laughed, tossing the blade of grass into the air, where it arced and caught the light. "Do you like it?" the Boy said, running thin fingers over his face. "I can be anyone I want, of course, but I thought this seemed fitting. Anyway, enough chitchat. Hop in." He patted the edge of the boat, sending water sloshing up the sides. The wood looked shiny and new, like it had just been polished. "You've got a prime opportunity here that most people don't get. I'd hate to see you waste it on me, when you could be with him. You want to go back home, don't you?"

Sam still didn't move. He couldn't decide if he was hallucinating or dreaming, but maybe it didn't matter. He was here, water lapping at his shoes, mosquitoes whispering across his skin. What did it matter if it was real or a dream?

He climbed in the canoe. The Boy grinned wider, and then he faded away. One second he was there, and the next second his body took on a shimmer, the sunlight cutting in one side and out the other. Then he dropped to the grass, body melting in a cascade of light, and a cat emerged in his place. One-Eye hopped in beside Sam, and the boat lurched suddenly, slicing a smooth path through the sheet of still water.

The strange part was that he hadn't found any paddles, yet the canoe moved steadily forward as if guided by an invisible string. But there was no time to wonder about that. Sam's chest swelled as he drew closer to the familiar dock overlooking the water, and the little white house, and the single can of Orange Crush sitting pristine and untouched, dew drops rolling down the bright orange aluminum.

"Am I really here?" Sam said, peering down at the cat that wasn't a cat. One-Eye cocked his head but didn't answer.

As they got closer to the dock, another sound mingled with the dancing leaves and the clinking wind chimes: whistling. Pa could whistle most any tune, note for note, as long as it had a good twang and was something worth listening to. His favorite was "Country Roads" by John Denver, because he said it reminded him of Mama. As soon as the whistling reached Sam's ears, he could barely stop himself from jumping out and swimming the rest of the way, but soon enough the canoe bumped gently against the edge of the dock.

Excited and confused and shaking something awful, he lifted himself out onto the damp, familiar wood. One-Eye leaped past him, landing like a spider and disappearing around the side of the house.

Sam followed the sound of whistling, though now the vibrations coming up from his belly were so strong he found it hard to walk without falling over. It had only been one day, but he already missed the creak of the decking under his feet and the smell of wood that only knew one way to be, and that was wet. He missed it all so much his body ached.

He came around to the front of the house and there, leaning against the porch railing like it was just any ordinary day, was Pa. The real Pa. He was holding the De Havilland bomber in one hand, only now it was shiny and whole, just like the day they'd put the finishing touches on it out in Pa's workshop. He turned it over in his hands, the fresh paint reflecting back the light. Sam felt in his pocket, but the broken propeller blade was gone.

Pa looked up and saw Sam, and the whistle died in his throat.

"There you are. 'Bout time you showed up," Pa said, and he flashed that familiar crooked smile, except it looked a whole lot better on him than on the other, younger Pa.

Sam blinked. He didn't even feel himself moving, but the next thing he knew he was squeezing Pa's chest, not even caring that his face was smushed into his sweaty armpit. Pa squeezed him back and then finally let go and held Sam out at arm's length. Sam wiped all the wet off his face and rubbed his eyes so he could get a good look at Pa and make sure he wasn't dreaming. But he wasn't, because he could feel Pa and smell him, and so surely that was proof.

"Something happen after school today?" Pa said. He looked down at Sam's hands, which were beat-up and bruised from the fight.

"It was nothing, Pa. Just roughhousing."

"Okay, if you say so." He stared at Sam a while longer, getting that little frown he sometimes got right between his eyes. "Seems like I haven't seen you in a while."

Sam stared, wondering suddenly how much Pa remembered. He chose his words carefully. "No, Pa, everything's fine. Better than fine, because you're here."

"Where else would I be?" He smiled, but it wasn't his usual smile, and he kept looking down at One-Eye and then back up at Sam like they were puzzle pieces, only he couldn't figure out where each one fit. "You sure everything's okay? You look . . ." Pa didn't finish.

"I'm fine, promise." Sam looked Pa over, his mind still racing and pinging. "How about you? You feel all right?"

Pa thought on this a while. He rubbed at his forehead, like he was expecting a headache, and then cracked his neck, but finally dropped his hands back down by his side. "Right as a rainstorm, as far as I can tell. Now, come on, let's go fly your plane a while. It's about time we tested out that new motor."

Sam didn't know what to say to this, because they'd tested that new motor months ago. Was it possible that Pa didn't remember? And if he'd forgotten that, then what else had he forgotten?

"You sure you're okay?" Pa said. "Because it looks to me like you're holding in a whole heap of trouble. Anything you need to tell me?"

Sam thought it over, which wasn't easy because just then One-Eye decided to start yowling and using Sam's jeans as a scratching post.

"Stop that, now. What's gotten into you?" Pa picked up that scraggly cat and studied him for a while. "Ain't that an odd one," he said, and his eyes took on a strange, dreamy quality. "He looks just like . . ." Pa trailed off, and after a while it was like his brain forgot all about being worried, and the next thing Sam knew, Pa was cradling that ugly cat like a baby. One-Eye collapsed into a puddle of jelly in Pa's arms. His head lolled back in contentment, but the look he gave Sam was still a nasty one.

"Come on, Pa. Let's go fly that plane."

That afternoon was one of the best of Sam's life. The shade and the swamp air and the feel of hot grass squishing under bare feet. Pa took off his boots too, and they stood side by side, elbows touching, peering up into the clouds.

Mostly, they flew.

The motor worked like a dream, just the way Sam

remembered. He held the controller while Pa whooped and hollered, watching the plane soar higher and higher, doing loop-the-loops and death-defying dives. The most exciting part was when Sam got to race a dragonfly, only it wasn't just any old dragonfly, but one even bigger than his plane, but thankfully not as fast. The De Havilland won with at least an inch to spare, at least that's the way Pa called it.

They stopped for a while to cool off, and boy, there was nothing better than sitting in the shade with Pa on a hot Bayou St. George day. Even One-Eye was kind of funny, though he was still creepy too, the way he kept chasing dragonflies, leaping straight up in the air like his butt was on a spring, flailing his skinny legs, spinning and twirling and always missing by at least a mile. The dragonflies seemed to be having fun too, especially the giant ones, because they kept dive-bombing One-Eye's bottom, and that old rag of a cat didn't act the least bit afraid.

"Can you believe him?" Pa said, laughing so hard he snorted. That made Sam laugh, too, and soon they were both bowled over, clutching their bellies. "And to think, Pops thought he should be put down."

One-Eye kept right on leaping and flailing and tumbling down in the grass, but Pa's laughter died in his throat. "But that was a long time ago now. That was before you were even . . ." He stopped and looked over at Sam, like maybe he was some kind of stranger and not his own son. The clouds shifted and shadows flitted across his eyes. "There's something wrong with me, ain't there?"

Suddenly, Sam's heart was pounding a million miles an hour in his chest. "No, Pa. Nothing's wrong with you. You're just confused." One-Eye stopped his jumping and settled down in front of Pa, watching him with his cool, silvery gaze.

"There was a car accident."

No, not that. Not now. "You don't have to worry about that, Pa. Not anymore. Let's just keep flying, or we could fish a while or—"

"Yeah, there was an accident. I heard the tires screech up ahead. It was raining, and I was riding my bike home from school. There was a hill, I remember, only it wasn't here, it was . . ."

Sam's mind worked overtime, trying to figure out what Pa was saying. "You mean back in Oklahoma?"

"That's right. I pedaled harder after I heard those tires squeal, and when I got to the top of the hill the car sped off, spraying me with gravel. I didn't see any other cars around, and I was about to head on home what with all the rain, but then I heard another sound. This kind of strangled crying, and I looked over in the grass and saw a smashed-up lump, all gray and covered in blood." He reached out and touched One-Eye's face, massaging the spot where his other eye should have been. "That blue-jay driver had run over half his face. I didn't know what to do, so I bundled him up in my jacket and rode as fast as I could to Doc Barbara's place."

Sam watched Pa's expression change as he drifted away into the memory. For a moment, he wasn't Pa anymore, but the boy Sam had seen in the picture on his bedside table, the one wearing dirty overalls and holding One-Eye in his arms, the one who'd greeted him inside the tree and turned into a cat and . . . Sam's mind started spinning. "She worked all night, stitching and pumping, and by the time the sun came up, that little cat looked like Frankenstein's monster, only a whole lot uglier."

One-Eye melted again, like he was more puddle than cat, and Pa set to rubbing his belly. "I thought for sure he'd never wake up, looking the way he did. I just knew he was dead and gone, and maybe it was my fault for not riding faster. But as soon as the medicine wore off, he blinked his one good eye and yowled something fierce, and then rolled onto his back spread-eagle, like he was asking for a tummy rub. That was the first time I knew that miracles really did happen; I wanted to name him that—Miracle—but every-one else kept calling him One-Eye, and I guess the name just stuck."

Once he was finished talking, Pa looked up at Sam. "I told you that story once, when you were little, but you wouldn't remember. It's funny, ain't it?"

"What, Pa?"

"The things we remember and the things we choose to forget." A cool breeze blew in, and Sam saw with a shiver how the sunlight was already disappearing behind the tree-tops. His brain was still spinning, thinking of One-Eye and the accident and . . . Pa. Did he really not remember that he was dead?

Pa's expression grew serious, the smile lines on either side of his mouth settling into deep, stony cracks. "That night, when I was driving home from the feed store and it started to rain . . ." Sam's heart seized in his chest. This was it. Like his thoughts had somehow triggered the memory in Pa and now his secret world would crumble around him. He wanted to shake Pa, to stop him from saying what came next, but his hands had turned to lead. "I didn't make it back, did I?"

"Pa—" Sam started to answer when he felt Pa's hand heavy on his shoulder.

"It's all right. Ever since you came here, I don't know, it's like I just woke up from a dream and I can't remember how I got here or why. I have all these memories rushing through my brain, and I keep trying to latch on, but they're too slippery, like catfish that keep dodging my hook. But I remember now. This isn't home, is it?" He watched a giant dragonfly buzz overhead, his wings as loud as car engines.

"Pa, don't." Sam took Pa's hand and squeezed, like maybe if he squeezed hard enough, Pa would stop talking.

"It's some other place, and I'm . . . I'm dead."

Sam didn't speak. He couldn't speak, so he just nodded and Pa hung his head. One-Eye had stopped wiggling, and now he stood apart, surveying them with his cold, silver glare.

Slowly, painfully, Pa turned his head to face Sam. "If you're here, does that mean you're dead too?"

"No." The idea came as such a shock, Sam nearly laughed. "I'm fine, Pa, promise. I found a tree, a doorway, and when I climbed through, here I was."

Pa stared at Sam in wonder. He touched Sam's chin with one rough hand. "Ain't that something."

"Sure is," Sam agreed.

Neither knew what else to say or do, considering the gravity of the situation, so finally Pa said, "That's enough flying for one day. What do you say we go catch some fish?"

Sam felt the tiny muscles in his jaw relax and his smile came back full force. He ran to the shed to grab the rods and tackle box. Everything looked just the same as before the accident and the big gray dumpster—the dusty shelves packed full of tools, old lures, cans of nails, a gator skull Pa found washed up on the shore, a twenty-four-pack of Orange Crush, Sam's tricycle from when he was a kid. Even the jar of gator teeth he and Pa had collected together, still whole and intact. It all smelled the same too, like oil and sawdust and wet wood.

"Got it!" He found Pa around the back of the house, legs dangling over the edge of the dock.

"'Bout time. Those fish aren't gonna catch themselves."

That was one of the things Pa always said, and Sam's face relaxed a little more. He dug up a few worms from the mud on the side of the dock, and they prepped their hooks and then cast their lines out into the deepest part of the swamp. They didn't say anything for a while, just soaking in the wonder of what was happening, but then Pa opened a fresh can of Orange Crush, and that crisp little pop was the best sound Sam had heard all year.

"Here you go," Pa said, handing Sam a warm soda.

Even though he preferred them cold, the syrupy liquid tasted better than he could have imagined. Kind of like drinking a popsicle that had melted in the sun—the sun, which, as they fished, was steadily dropping down behind the trees, casting the swamp and the tiny white house and Pa's weatherworn face in a soft amber glow.

"How does it feel?" Sam said after a while. "Being . . ."

Pa didn't answer right away. He took his time sipping on his drink and running his tongue between the gap in his front teeth. "Don't hurt, if that's what you mean." That crooked smile. The one that said everything's right and fine and just the way it should be. But how could it be?

"How much do you remember?"

Pa turned his gaze out to face the swamp and the brigades of giant dragonflies patrolling the surface. "Not much. One minute I was headed home from the feed store, next minute the sky opened up and even Noah himself would've swore at the sight of all that rain. Big, thick curtains of it battering the Sunbird. Then the hail. It was a miracle the windshield didn't break. That was a mighty fine car, but it wasn't made for storm season. Then I tried to pull over, wait it out, but I must've picked the wrong spot, because the next thing I knew I was sliding."

Sam stopped breathing. He wanted Pa to shut up, to stop talking like he'd driven into a ditch and died, but the other part of him needed to know.

"What else do you remember?"

Pa looked over at Sam, watching him the way he sometimes did with his bright, almost golden eyes. "That's it. After that, I woke up here. Except, my memory wasn't so good, so it was more like I'd never left. At first, I remember this glow, like someone parked their car out front in the trees, and they were shining their high beams. After a bit, the lights faded, and I just, I don't know . . . I was here, but I wasn't. Time kind of stalled out—until you came, at least."

Sam watched Pa's face in the fading light. He was Pa, no question, but there was something different about him too. Something Sam had never seen before on Pa's face: fear.

A rustling came from behind, and One-Eye leaped over

Sam's head and landed atop the post at the edge of the dock. Shadows settled into the harsh folds of his face, and Sam did his best to ignore him. He looked over at Pa and saw that Pa was also watching the cat.

"He's not my One-Eye, is he?"

Sam didn't know. One-Eye set to licking his sharp claws, and Sam returned his gaze to Pa. In the orangey predusk light, Pa's body seemed to ripple, like looking at an image reflected in water.

"Man, it sure is getting dark," Pa said. "Seems too early for sunset." He was right. Sam watched the last strands of sun dip below the tupelo trees, only how could it be getting dark this early in the afternoon?

Something moved out of the corner of Sam's eye, and he turned toward the cat. Only he wasn't a cat anymore, but the Boy, the young version of Pa, sitting atop the post with one leg crossed over the other, tapping his Hamilton Aviaton watch.

"Almost time to go," the Boy said. He grinned, only this time it didn't remind him of Pa at all. His mouth was full of small, razor-sharp teeth.

Pa gaped at the Boy, because it must have been strange staring himself in the face, but then something out in the swamp caught his attention. At this late hour, the swamp had turned to a sheet of black marble, lit only by the occasional passing lightning bug. These were normal size, but they glowed an eerie shade of blue-green. Sam and Pa watched as a ripple broke the surface followed by a pair of glowing yellow eyes.

"Come on up here," Pa said, real quiet, and he gripped Sam's arm and half pulled him up so his legs weren't dangling over the side.

"Is that the Colonel?" Sam said, a combined jolt of fear and excitement lighting up his chest. The Colonel was a legend in Bayou St. George. People said he was a demon gator, on account of him living over sixty years without ever being caught. People said he could leap straight up in the air and snatch an owl out of a tree if he wanted. They said he'd once snapped a tour boat in half with a single bite, and no bullet or arrow could kill him.

"Sure looks like him, only . . ."

Pa didn't finish, and Sam thought he knew why. He'd seen glimpses of the Colonel before, four or five times, since hunting down the Colonel was Pa's second-favorite pastime, after fishing, but he'd never seen him like this— the crusty sores around his eyes or the deep cuts along his snout or the arrow shaft sprouting from his skull like a unicorn's horn, only covered in blood.

The Boy on the post hissed and bared his teeth as the Colonel swam closer, stopping right in front of the dock. Pa tightened his grip on Sam's arm, looking from the strange boy to the gator and back again.

The swamp went dead quiet, their bobbers still rocking on the eerily calm surface.

Then, without warning, the Colonel lunged, water spraying, his massive body surging through the air straight toward them. Wood cracked, two-inch-long nails scrabbled on the decking, and Pa thrust Sam back behind him quick, shouting, "Stay away!"

But in the end, it didn't matter, because the Colonel changed direction at the last second, jerking to the right in midair, his jaws aiming not for Sam or Pa but the Boy.

"Watch out!" Sam shouted. The Boy might be a total creep, but Sam still had to warn him. It was no use. In the split second it took the Colonel to change direction, the Boy had gone. Disappeared. The Colonel's jaws clamped down on the empty post, splinters flying.

Without warning, a force even stronger than the Colonel's jaws wrenched Sam free from Pa's grasp.

"Sam!" Pa lunged, grabbing hold of Sam's arm, but the force was too strong. It picked him up, like an invisible tornado, and for one frozen moment, he was floating, Pa's grip the only thing stopping him from flying clean away. He could see Pa screaming and hear the Colonel scraping at the dock, and then Pa got hold of his other arm, and he started to reel Sam in like the world's biggest fish, but then the tornado flexed its muscles and ripped Sam free.

"Come back!" Pa called, but it was too late. Sam was

hurtling across the water and onto the far shore, his body slapping into vines and tufts of Spanish moss. Before he could scream, the same invisible force pulled him back into the tree, and he was shooting up a dark tunnel, raw wood cutting his skin, dark shapes speeding past, leaves slashing his face.

Flying up and up.

And then, suddenly, light sliced open his vision and he hit the ground hard, his brain ringing in his ears. He struggled to his feet, spinning around, reaching for Pa, but all he found was grass and a gravel road and a grape-soda tree covered once again in dead bark.

"Pa!"

He thrust his head into the hollow only to crack his skull on solid wood. "No!" He tore at the back of the hole with his fingernails, wedging splinters deeper and deeper under his skin. When that didn't work, he kicked the tree and didn't stop.

He was so busy kicking and clawing that he didn't hear tires crunching over the gravel. Strong arms circled around him and squeezed him tight, and even though he turned around and kicked Aunt Jo hard in the shin, she didn't let go.

7

"AUNT JO, HE'S IN THERE. It's Pa. He's . . ." Sam couldn't finish, and Aunt Jo gave him a look like he'd reached down deep in her gut and squeezed.

He freed himself from her death grip and looked out at the tree and the dirty gravel road, brain reeling. He saw the remnants of his plane lying on the grass, just the way he'd left them. He slid numb fingers into his pocket and felt the edge of the broken propeller blade.

"Come on. Let's get you home." She picked up the pieces of his plane and stood there looking small for maybe the first time in her whole life. She opened her mouth, like she wanted to offer him some comforting words, but then closed it again.

Behind them, wind rattled the dead branches. Sam didn't want to leave; he couldn't. But the hollow was sealed. He could see the back of the hole from where he was standing, and the plane . . . But it had been real. It hadn't been like one of Pa's stories. And Pa had held on, trying to keep him there. He had to go back.

What was it the Boy had said? That the doorway wouldn't

stay open all night. Maybe that meant it would open again. He shook his head hard, trying to organize his thoughts, but they wouldn't connect. None of it made any sense.

He wanted to fight, to punch Aunt Jo for real if he had to, but suddenly he was more exhausted than he'd ever been in his life. He let Aunt Jo lead him to the car. As soon as they got inside, it started to rain. The rain came up fast and sudden, pounding the little car so hard they could barely move against the force of all that wind and water. So much for the purple-haired girl's story about Holler never getting any rain. Aunt Jo had her positive affirmations cranked all the way up, but she turned them down and they listened to the rain instead.

After a rough drive, they pulled up to the yellow dollhouse and sat in the car. The wind rocked them back and forth, like they were on a boat instead of dry land. Sam turned around and saw his bag in the back seat, which meant that Aunt Jo knew about the fight. For the first time since it had happened, Sam looked down at his right hand. His knuckles were bloody and the back of his hand was one big purple bruise, even worse than yesterday's fight with the dumpster. He stretched out his fingers and made a fist, sliding it in his pocket so Aunt Jo wouldn't notice. Inside he winced, but it wasn't because of the pain.

It's because it never happened, said a slithery voice inside his head. *It was all a dream. Your pa's dead, or did you forget?*

91

Worms are crawling out of his eye sockets, not dangling from the end of his lure.

"Shut up."

"What's that?" Aunt Jo snapped him out of his ugly thoughts, looking like maybe he really had punched her in the face.

"Nothing."

They sat in silence for a while longer, waiting for the rain to die down. It wasn't the comfortable kind of silence, like when he was out fishing with Pa. It was the kind of silence that made him itch under his skin.

"Strange, us getting all this rain," Aunt Jo said. "I don't remember anything on the weather reports." Silence. "Oh, I almost forgot to tell you, I bought cake."

Of all the pointless things in the world to say, Sam thought that was probably the most pointless. He could tell it was his turn to speak, because the itching under his skin got so bad he half wanted to peel it off, but what could he say to something pointless like that? Especially when Pa was out there somewhere, waiting for him.

"Caramel Dream from Gina's Diner. That was your pa's favorite."

Her words sucked all the air out of the car. Sam opened the door and made a run for the porch, the broken plane parts still cradled in his hoodie. Aunt Jo got out too, but she stopped for his backpack, which was heavier than it looked, and by the time she made it to the porch she looked more like a fish than an old lady.

He couldn't help it. He tried the cake. Even though he hated himself for doing it, and even though the box was one big, soggy mess, the cake actually turned out to be pretty good.

It had this gooey caramel filling, big globs of frosting, and chocolate caramel candies on top that melted on your tongue. He ate it real slow, the whole time thinking he shouldn't, but he knew Pa wouldn't turn down cake even if the world ended and the zombies started eating people's faces off. That thought made Sam feel a little better. Not the world ending, but the thought of Pa telling another one of his stories about zombies or swamp monsters or chasing down the Colonel.

"How is it?" Aunt Jo said. She had barely touched her piece, but Sam's was nearly finished.

"It's all right."

"That's good." She pushed her cake around on her plate, and that was when she noticed the cuts on Sam's hands.

"Mr. Redding said you got in a fight, but I didn't know it was that bad." Sam tried to resist her, but she marched him to the sink and refused to let go until she'd washed and bandaged both of his hands. "When did you plan on telling me about what happened at school?"

Sam didn't answer, and it was clear Aunt Jo wasn't about

to budge, so instead he asked, "Can I go up to my room?"

Aunt Jo took a long time considering, puffing herself up and giving him some serious evil eye that might have worked okay in the army, but it wouldn't work on him.

"Fine, if that's what you want."

He stood up too fast, and the chair would have toppled over if he hadn't caught it.

"Don't worry about the dishes."

"Okay." He looked over at the pieces of his plane. He'd dumped them under the hall table when he came inside. He thought about picking them up and taking them to his room, but what was the point? "Thanks for the cake or whatever."

Aunt Jo didn't say anything until he'd already started climbing the steps. "Sam, wait. I think we need to talk."

Great, here it was. The big speech about not fighting, even though that kid he'd punched was obviously some blue jay who totally deserved it. And he was the one with a broken plane and fingers that could barely hold a fork and, besides, who cared, because Pa was dead, but he wasn't.

He walked back down the steps and stared at his shoelaces. The worst part was, even though he was staring at his shoelaces, he kept seeing Pa's face, and Pa was giving him the same look he'd given Sam the day he'd laughed at the neighbor kid for crashing on his bike. That kid ended up becoming Sam's best friend, until he moved away, and the reason he'd crashed

94

was because he had an inner ear infection and couldn't help it. Sam had felt like the jerk of the world when he found out, and he hadn't even meant to laugh, not really, but the worst part had been the crinkly look of disappointment on Pa's face when he'd done it. That look made him just about melt on the spot and never want to get up again.

"I want you to know why I was gone all those years."

Sam looked up at Aunt Jo and their eyes met. It was maybe the first time he'd really looked at her since everything that had happened. She drew in a deep breath, and now she was the one who looked away, staring at her hands that lay palms-down on the table. "I never wanted to stay away, but the truth is . . . your pa asked me to. He had every right to do it, but I want you to know that I would have come around more often if I could have."

Sam let the words sink in. "So it's Pa's fault that we didn't see you for four years?"

"No, listen. I want to explain, it's just not the type of thing that's easy to talk about."

"You're lying." Heat crept up the back of Sam's neck, making the edges of the room go blurry.

"Sam." She sat there looking small, and Sam wondered again what it would be like to punch her for real, in the face.

"Pa wouldn't do that. You didn't know him at all. Just because you grew up together, you think you know everything, but you don't. I bet he hated that gross cake."

"Just listen."

"I'm going to bed." Sam pounded up the stairs before he really did hit something or someone, shaking away the image of Pa's crinkly, disappointed face.

"It's not even five o'clock," Aunt Jo called, and he heard her chair squeak just before he slammed his bedroom door.

He didn't mean to fall asleep. He wanted to go find Pa, despite the pounding rain and the closed-up hollow and every grape-soda thing that had happened since he'd left Bayou St. George, but the long day dragged him down. Soon, he was snoring into his pillow. He didn't notice before closing his eyes that it was covered in cat hair, and he didn't hear later when cars began to pull up outside and the front door opened and closed, letting in the smell of moldy air.

In his sleep, Sam was busy struggling against a monstrous gator with hooks for teeth and a devil's horn sprouting right out of his skull. He'd managed to pin him on the dock when his shape changed and he was Pa, then he changed again and he was the Colonel.

They rolled over the edge of the dock, dropping into the murky, green water. A moment later, Sam shot up in bed, sputtering.

It took him a minute to figure out where he was and

that the gator wrestling had been nothing but a dream. Slowly, his breath calmed down. Sweat stung his armpits and dripped down the front of his shirt. He rubbed his temple, trying to remember more about his dream, but all he could see when he closed his eyes was the disappointed look on Pa's face.

Great.

Even though he didn't want to, even though it wasn't his fault Aunt Jo had gone missing all that time and then tried to make it up to him with total grape-soda-flavored cake, he knew he had to go downstairs and say something. It's what Pa would have wanted. He wasn't ready to call it an apology, not yet, but he'd say just about anything to wipe that look of disappointment off Pa's face, even if it was only in his head.

He'd already tiptoed to the end of the hall before he noticed the voices down below. He couldn't see anybody from where he stood, just the front door and part of the kitchen, but he heard someone talking like they were giving a speech and chairs creaking and someone else coughing and clearing their throat.

He leaned over the railing to try to get a look in the living room, but this guy in overalls and a ball cap walked past. The guy stopped and stared, like maybe Sam was the one who shouldn't be there.

"Hey," the guy said, but he was too late because Sam

slipped into the first room he found and shut the door.

The room smelled like Aspercreme and flowery air freshener. He was in Aunt Jo's bedroom.

He tested out the edge of her pointy mattress. It wasn't really made of wood, but this weird foam that formed to the shape of his butt. Gross. Listening for footsteps on the stairs, he studied the picture frames on the dresser. Lots of him and Pa, going all the way back to when Sam was a baby. A few of Aunt Jo posing in her military uniform next to the planes she used to fly. Sam remembered sitting with his chin on Aunt Jo's knees when he was little, listening to her describe what it felt like to fly a plane as it broke through the clouds.

She was the whole reason he liked planes in the first place. Her and Pops, who had once been a real-life flying ace in World War II. When he was little, he'd wanted to be a pilot when he grew up. And now? Now he didn't want to be anything at all.

Other than the bed and the dresser, the room was pretty much empty. She had her own bathroom, with deodorant and lotion and toothpaste all lined up in a row. There was the chair in the corner with the stack of scratchy blankets and an old rug that was starting to unravel.

He knew Pa didn't approve of snooping, but somehow his fingers found the knob on the top dresser drawer, and since he was already there, he figured he might as well open it. It was filled with white tube socks and huge granny underwear. He closed that one up fast and tried the next one. He found piles of loose photos, rolls of pennies, three army medals in wooden boxes, a stack of Christmas cards Sam had drawn with these ugly red-eyed Santas, and a tin full of poker chips, just like the one Aunt Jo wore around her neck. Except these weren't regular poker chips, like the kind Pa brought out whenever his buddies came over for a game. They had dates on the front—thirty days, sixty days, three months, all the way up to one year.

Sam closed that drawer and opened the big one below it. Even though he knew what it was, it still took him by surprise. It was a leg. There was this hard plastic part on top, where the end of your leg would go, and then a metal hinge for a knee with two plastic sensors and a piece of curved, bouncy plastic instead of a foot, like the ones Olympic athletes sometimes wore on TV. Maybe this was the leg Aunt Jo used for running. It even had a charger so you could plug it into the wall. Sam touched it and shivers ran up his fingertips. Suddenly he thought about the feeling he'd had seeing that blue jay of a kid touch his stuff. He was doing the same thing, only maybe it was worse because touching that artificial leg felt kind of like touching a real one.

He shut the drawer and slipped back out into the hallway. The people downstairs were applauding. Sam had started back to his room when someone said, "Hi."

The purple-haired girl was staring up at him from the bottom of the stairs.

"Hi," Sam said.

"You got your stuff back."

It took him a minute to realize that she was talking about his backpack, which was still sitting in the front hall where he'd left it.

"Yeah."

"That's good. Those guys were total jerks."

"Yeah."

She adjusted her glasses, which was a thing he noticed she did a lot, and he had this weird urge to tell her she looked pretty with her glasses on, but he didn't, because that would be weird and, besides, why would he?

"Are you coming downstairs?"

He came downstairs. There were maybe fifteen people sitting on folding chairs in the living room. Aunt Jo stood at the front, and she was busy saying something about surrendering to a higher power and living life one day at a time, so she didn't see him.

"There's cake," the girl said. They went in the kitchen and sat at the table, where Aunt Jo had not one but four different cakes, each with a few slices missing. And here he was thinking she'd bought the cake just for him. "That's the best thing about these meetings. The desserts."

They sat at the table and she cut herself a slice of Caramel

Dream. "You want some?"

"Um, no thanks."

"You should really try it. It's like eating a cloud, if clouds had caramel filling and were made of chocolate."

Sam laughed, and the girl looked up like maybe she thought he was laughing at her, which he was, but not in a bad way. "Maybe just a little piece." He sliced off the smallest piece he could and took a bite. "You're right. It tastes exactly like clouds."

Now she laughed too, and he thought her laugh was kind of pretty, like beer cans clinking together in the wind, only not really. She took another bite of cake. He sat there staring at his piece, trying hard to think of something to say, but even though it was quiet, it was a Pa kind of quiet, nice and comfortable, except he was pretty sure he was sweating through the armpits of his shirt.

"You like planes?" she said, once she was done chewing. "My dad gets sick every time he flies, like barfing into a bag sick, which I guess is why he doesn't visit."

"Oh, sorry. Maybe you can visit him sometime?"

The girl looked down at her plate and didn't answer. She'd eaten all the caramel filling part, so now all she had was a floppy shell of chocolate cake.

"Yeah, maybe. He lives in California, though. It's really expensive to fly there."

"True. That's the worst." Sam wanted to say that having

a dad in California was actually a lot better than not having a dad at all, but he didn't. The girl dug her fork into her cake, tearing off tiny chunks but not eating them.

"Hey, I don't even know your name."

"It's Edie."

"Sam."

"I know." She laughed, but he could tell it wasn't a mean laugh, and it really did sound like Pa's wind chimes only a whole lot better.

"So why are you here?" he said, and then he realized that maybe that sounded rude, but Edie didn't seem to notice.

"For the meeting. Your aunt pays me to pass out cake and help clean up, stuff like that. My mom used to come to the meetings, too, but now she mostly stays home."

"What meetings?"

Edie studied him through her glasses, which were super cute and matched her hair, just like her sunglasses. But so what? It's not like he really noticed.

"You know, NA." She must have seen the way he was staring at her, like he was trying to figure out why his aunt would start a club with such a terrible name, and so she said, "Narcotics Anonymous. For people who have a problem with addiction. Your aunt started holding meetings a few years ago."

"Like a club for drug addicts?"

"No." Edie lowered her voice, her eyes darting to the

102

living room. Everyone in the other room had gone quiet, like maybe they'd heard what he said, but then a chair squeaked and someone started talking again. "I mean, yes, technically, but mostly it's a club for people in recovery. Like your aunt."

"So they are drug addicts? Even my aunt?" This time he made sure to say it quiet, but it was pretty hard, considering. No wonder Pa had asked Aunt Jo to stay away. Drugs did horrible stuff to your body and could even make you hurt people. Like in that video they'd made him watch last year in health class.

"She's in recovery, which means she's trying to get better." Edie didn't sound angry, but she kept stabbing at her hollowed-out cake, turning the brown bits to mush. "Besides, she just got her one-year chip last month, which is a big deal. Your aunt's a hero around here. If it weren't for her, a lot of these people wouldn't have anywhere else to turn."

Sam was trying to understand, but it was a lot to take in. "That's what all those chips are for?"

"What do you mean?"

"I found all these chips in her room, um, accidentally, and I thought they were just weird poker chips."

"They give them out at the end of every meeting. They're to show how long each person's been clean."

"I can't believe this. What kind of drugs is she on?"

"She's not on anything, not anymore. And just because she has an addiction, doesn't mean your aunt's a bad person. It's like an illness. Regular people have problems with addiction all the time. Good people."

"Really. Name one."

Edie looked down and went back to smashing her cake. She didn't say anything for a while, and so he heard what Aunt Jo said next. Her booming voice carried all the way from the living room.

"Four years ago, when I thought I'd lost everything, I decided to open up my home. If I'd known that you misfits were planning to show up, I might have changed my mind." Everybody laughed, like she'd just made the best joke in the whole world. "I thought I'd hit rock bottom. I lost my leg and my first love, flying. I'd never been any good at sitting behind a desk, and then I lost that job, too, because of the pills. I told myself I couldn't get any lower, and then I did something I'll never forgive myself for. I lost my family too."

The room got quiet, so quiet Sam could hear his breath loud in his ears. "That was when I knew I had to do something, to take control of my life. It's been a long road, but now I'm thirteen months clean and counting." Everyone applauded, even Edie. Sam kept his hands firmly in his lap.

"That's enough talk and tears for one night," she said. "There's cake in the kitchen and, first-timers, don't forget to pick up your chips."

"Where are you going?" Edie said, since Sam had abandoned his plate and was already heading back upstairs.

Of course, Aunt Jo came into the kitchen at that very same moment. He could tell she knew that he knew, and he tried to think of something to say, but what? What? The worst part was that she didn't look like a drug addict, she looked like the same Aunt Jo who used to drive down to Louisiana every year on his birthday to take him to the aviation museum.

"You can help me serve the cake," Edie said.

Sam hesitated. Pa's face floated behind his eyes, all crinkly and disappointed. Edie did that nervous thing with her glasses, which made him smile despite all the blue-jay thoughts racing around in his brain.

"Maybe. Just for a few minutes."

He found a big metal spatula and started plopping slices down on plates. He didn't look at Aunt Jo, and she didn't push him. While she dug around in the fridge for more juice, Sam got interrupted in his serving duties, since pretty much everybody in the room wanted to stop and shake his hand.

"Glad to meet ya, Sammy." The man in overalls and a ball cap gave him a big pat on the back after nearly crushing his hand. "I've been hearing about you since you were in diapers. Remember that time you peed in the Grand

Canyon? We all laughed when your aunt told us that one. Fine lady, your aunt. Real keeper."

A woman with gold strands woven into her braids hugged him so hard she nearly squeezed the life out of him. "Your auntie's a survivor, and that means you are too. Just remember that your dad's in a better place. Trust in that higher power, you hear?"

It went on and on, until finally the last car drove away and it was just him and Edie and Aunt Jo, along with a whole bunch of dirty plates. Sam was so tired and sore from all that shaking he thought he could sleep for a week.

"How about I order some pizza for dinner so we don't make any more dishes?" Aunt Jo looked at Sam, and suddenly he felt the quiet of the empty house settling on his shoulders.

"If you want. It's your house." He swallowed, trying to decide if he was angry or nervous or something in between.

He helped Edie with the dishes while Aunt Jo ordered two large pizzas with pepperoni, pineapple, and extra cheese. He washed while Edie dried. With the water running, he didn't have to say anything, which was good, because he didn't know what to say about NA or Aunt Jo's words or the fact that everybody thought she was some kind of hero.

Maybe he didn't hate her as much as before, now that he understood more about why she'd stayed away. And if Edie was right, about addiction being an illness, then maybe it

106

was a good thing that Aunt Jo was getting help. But it didn't change anything. Or even if it did change things, just a little, he didn't know what to do about it.

"You washed that fork three times." He looked over to see Edie smiling at him. Jesus, Mary, and Joseph, that smile.

"Sorry." He turned off the water and handed her the fork.

"I think that's the last of it."

"Finally."

Aunt Jo finished wiping off the table and appraised their work. "That's a mighty fine job if I ever saw one. You two make a good team." Sam felt heat creep into his face and wished it back down again. "Now," she said, rubbing her hands together. "How about some cake?"

Edie laughed, and even though it was a pretty terrible joke, Sam laughed too. At least a little. On the inside.

When the pizza came, Sam grabbed a slice and took a huge bite. It tasted okay at first, until he thought about how pepperoni and pineapple was Pa's favorite and how it wasn't fair that he could have some but Pa couldn't.

"You only ate one bite," Edie said.

"I'll save the rest for breakfast."

Aunt Jo thought that was funny, because Pa used to eat cold pizza for breakfast, too, when he was a kid, which made Sam never want to eat pizza again in his whole grape-soda life. Because none of it was fair, and he suddenly felt bad for eating any pizza at all and vowed that this would be the last time.

Dinner wasn't that awful, though, because Edie told these funny stories about her science-fair project, which was a solar-powered glider, and how she'd accidentally knocked two of the letters off the school sign so it read *Goo uck Wildcats* instead of *Good Luck Wildcats*.

When they were done eating, Aunt Jo gave Edie an entire pizza to take home. "I know your mom doesn't like pineapple, but she can pick it off." Aunt Jo winked.

"Oh, I don't think she's home. She went to visit her sister for a few days."

"In Tulsa?"

"Yeah, but she'll be back on Saturday. Maybe sooner."

It was Thursday.

"And she left you home all by yourself?" Sam could tell Aunt Jo was trying not to sound mad, but he didn't think she was mad at Edie.

Edie didn't answer.

"That's it, you're staying with us. This house has too many empty rooms as it is."

"It's really okay. I'm fine by myself."

"Well, I'm not."

Aunt Jo bustled around grabbing blankets and towels and a brand-new toothbrush, which, by the way, she seemed to have a lot of. Edie just stood in the hall looking kind of mortified, and Sam didn't know what to say, so he just stood there, too, wishing he had a brain that knew how to make words instead of a grape-soda brain that turned to mush anytime something important happened.

"I bet I could fix that," Edie said.

Sam had no idea what she was talking about, until she picked up one of the pieces of his plane, which were still under the hall table where he'd left them. She spun the broken propeller.

"Don't worry about it. It's just trash."

Edie studied the plane for a while and then set it down carefully on the floor. "My dad was good at fixing stuff. Once, he stayed up all night fixing this robot puppy I'd gotten for my birthday." She smiled at the memory. "That was forever ago, though, when I was, like, five."

Sam wondered how she could talk about her dad without getting angry at him for leaving. If his dad had moved away, he thought he'd take more than a few years to get over it.

"All set," Aunt Jo said, handing Edie a giant stack of blankets. "In case you get cold."

"I'll be fine," Edie said, her voice muffled by all the fuzzy fleece.

"The guest room's through here, this way." Aunt Jo guided Edie to a doorway under the stairs, which opened onto a tiny room with a cozy bed, side table, and lamp. "This used to be Pops's study."

Edie dropped the blankets onto the bed. There were probably enough to keep her warm through an entire Arctic winter.

"Thanks, Miss J," Edie said.

"Anytime, Miss E. Oh, and I almost forgot this." To Sam's horror, she reached into her blouse and pulled a ten dollar bill from her bra. "For helping out tonight. You got a safe place to keep this?"

"Yes, ma'am."

"Good girl. Now get some rest, and I'll drive you to school in the morning."

Aunt Jo left, and Sam was stuck standing there with his grape-soda brain that had forgotten how to make words.

"So, um, I guess I'll see you in the morning," Edie said.

"Yeah, okay."

He still didn't leave, because maybe his feet had stopped working along with his brain.

"Is your mom gone a lot?" The words kind of spilled out, and then right away he wished he hadn't said them.

"Pretty much."

"Oh, sorry."

"It's okay. Miss J just worries."

"Miss J?"

"Yeah, that's what a lot of people call her around here."

Sam tried looking Edie in the eyes, but it was kind of like staring straight at an eclipse without those ugly paper

110

glasses. He looked away.

"It's been hard for her."

"Because of your dad?"

"Because of everything. Mom's . . . I don't know, she tries, but . . . sometimes it's easier when she's not here."

"Oh."

Sam felt a hand on his shoulder and turned around to find Aunt Jo. "You two better get some sleep. Baby Girl leaves at eight-fifteen sharp."

"Good night," Edie said.

Her door clicked shut. Sam headed to his room, but Aunt Jo stopped him at the bottom of the stairs. "About today at school. I talked to Principal Everett, and he's letting you off with a warning. Everybody understands that you're going through a tough time."

She waited for him to say something. He could feel her waiting, and he wanted to say something, but once again, brain: mush.

"I guess you figured out tonight where I was for the last four years." Sam stole a look at Aunt Jo's cracked-leather face. Maybe she didn't look that different from the woman in those old photos, the one who used to burp him and drive him to a haunted house every other Halloween. "I wanted to tell you, to explain, but your pa . . . well, none of that matters now. What matters is that you're here and we're family."

She pulled Sam into a hug, and he didn't fight it. Once she let him go, he opened his mouth, trying to make some words come out, to say what was on his mind, but nothing happened. After a while, Aunt Jo gave his shoulder a squeeze. He watched her walk up the stairs, moving more slowly than she had the night before, and then she went in her room and closed the door.

That night, Sam turned all the lights off and sat on the windowsill in his bedroom, staring out at the shadows. He waited for one to peel itself away from the others and take the form of a cat or a boy or maybe a creepy spider. The rain had stopped a while back, but moisture still glittered on the dark grass, lit by strands of moonlight.

His first thought was, *So much for it never raining in Holler, Oklahoma.*

His second thought was, *If Pa was really out there, trapped inside some grape-soda tree, then what was he doing here staring at nothing?* He should go, sneak out while Aunt Jo was asleep and find a way to make the tree open. He slid the window up an inch, cringing at the scream of metal on metal. Crap. It was no use. After that morning, he knew he wouldn't have the guts to jump. He'd just have to go out the front, and then? Then he'd have to walk. So now what?

Something made a shiver run down Sam's spine. He turned to see the strange boy shimmering in the doorway.

He was resting one hand on the wall, and using the other to chew on a long blade of grass.

"I like your moxie, kid, I do, but you've got the timing all wrong." The Boy's eyes glinted in the moonlight, and they didn't look like Pa's anymore, but like the cat's. "See, the doorway won't open again until tomorrow. Once a day, at 3:45 p.m. on the dot. That's the deal. And even that deal won't last long."

Sam had a sudden urge to rush the Boy. He pictured his fist sinking into his grape-soda stomach, but he forced himself to stay still. "What do you know about it? Who are you anyway?"

"Me?" The corner of his lip curled up, revealing those same short, needle-thin teeth. "Just a friend. And you can trust me when I say that there's no way to force the tree open, not until the appointed time."

"The time Pa died?" Sam said, the words catching in his throat.

"That's right. Poetic, don't you think?"

What Sam thought was that he'd had enough. "Why are you here?"

"Like I said, I'm a friend."

"I didn't ask for a friend."

"But you need one." The Boy's eyes hardened into two polished marbles, sucking up all the light.

113

Sam thought of what had happened with Pa and the Colonel, and how the Colonel had shifted midair to go after the Boy.

"Go. I don't want you here."

The Boy's smile widened, revealing a darkness between his teeth even blacker than the surrounding shadows.

"As you wish."

He winked, and then his body quivered before bursting into a cloud of silver dust that vanished as soon as it had appeared. Numb, Sam crossed the room and picked up the single blade of grass, the only evidence of the Boy's visit. He ran it through his fingers and found that it was still wet on one end. He shuddered, standing frozen, staring at the space where the Boy had been.

When he finally crawled into bed a while later, he couldn't sleep. Frenzied thoughts kept zipping through his brain. Thoughts like giant dragonflies with sharp legs and veiny, motorized wings.

8

COLD PINEAPPLE AND PEPPERONI PIZZA probably doesn't seem like the best breakfast in the world, but it really was, especially when it had an extra-thick layer of congealed cheese. Sam might not have been hungry the night before, but now he couldn't seem to stop eating. Even if he still felt bad that he could eat and Pa couldn't. With each slice he consumed, Edie's eyes got wider.

"Are you sure all that cheese won't make you puke?"

"Nope." He took another huge bite and Edie laughed. It was a good sound, a Bayou St. George kind of sound. The night before, he thought he'd never eat pizza again, but hunger had a way of changing his mind. He hoped Pa would understand.

On the way to school, things were almost kind of normal, except that he spent the whole day itching to see Pa. To start, Aunt Jo turned on real music instead of her annoying positive affirmations, and the ride only took ten minutes instead of an hour, because they didn't have to wind all the way across town like they did on the bus.

Even his meeting with Principal Everett didn't turn out that bad. All he had to do was sit there in a chair next to Aunt Jo and nod every once in a while and pretend to look sorry. He even felt kind of bad for Joey Dunkirk, the kid who took his stuff, even if he was the biggest blue jay in America. His mom kept shouting in his ear and spit kept flying from her mouth and landing on Joey's face. Joey didn't seem to notice, since he was too busy being yelled at, but gross.

Once it was over, he and Joey shook hands and that was that. Joey sped right out of there, probably so he didn't have to get spit on anymore.

"Hang on, I almost forgot," Aunt Jo said. She reached into her purse and pulled out a padlock. "For your locker."

"Thanks."

The padlock was cold and heavy in his palm. He thought about saying sorry for being such a blue jay the whole past week, but Principal Everett was sitting right there, and besides, he still wasn't sure he was sorry.

"I guess I'll see you later," Sam said.

"Pick you up after school?" Aunt Jo asked.

"Um, yeah, sure." He didn't want to lie to Aunt Jo, but what else could he say? No way he could tell her the truth about Pa and the tree.

When he got to class it turned out that Mr. Redding had removed some of the extra desks and now everyone had assigned seats with little paper name plates. Sam's desk was all the way at the front, right by Mr. Redding.

Great.

At least he was still by the window.

He wasn't surprised to find that Joey Dunkirk was sitting on the opposite side of the room, back by the pencil sharpener. He found Edie, stuck in the middle, and she waved at him with her name plate. She'd drawn this weird monster in the corner with a diaper and blood shooting from its mouth. It was both creepy and hilarious, two of Sam's favorite things. He wondered what Mr. Redding would say if he saw it.

They spent most of the morning talking about owls, where they lived and what they ate, and then Mr. Redding brought out a big box filled with owl pellets, which turned out to be these dry, egg-shaped throw-ups that owls barf out when they're done eating. They each got a pair of tweezers and a piece of black paper, and their job was to pick out all the bones and try to guess what animal they'd come from. It was pretty great.

Everybody got really into it, and they were talking and laughing, and Sam didn't even care that nobody was talking to him. After a while, he wasn't even in the classroom anymore, but back on the tiny beach by their house, digging up shells and alligator teeth with Pa. One of Pa's grand ambitions was to have a photo featured in *Bobby Joe's Catch of the*

Week, which was this newsletter that Bobby Joe from the tackle shop put out, featuring all the biggest catches and most unusual finds around Bayou St. George.

Sam's picture had been in there once, that time he'd found an alligator skull the size of his thumb. Sometimes, the smallest stuff got featured too. Pa had been so proud he'd smiled for a week straight, but Sam knew that Pa wanted his picture in there one day too. And not just any picture. He wanted to be the first person in Bayou St. George history to capture a photo of the notorious Colonel. Now that would never happen.

Sam heard a snap. He'd cracked a piece of skull without even realizing it. He opened his tweezers and the finger-nail-size fragments dropped to his paper towel. Oh well. It wasn't like he could make a full skeleton anyway. All these bones seemed to have come from different animals, and they were hiding in a wad of dirty fur and feathers.

He set the tweezers down and looked out the window. It was the kind of bright spring day when the grass looks warm and you want to stay outside forever, basking in the sun. Of course, he was stuck inside. A metallic twinkle caught his eye from inside the nearby clump of bushes. He watched as the bushes shook and shivered and a gray shape emerged from the center, settling itself on the grass.

It was One-Eye.

The cat or the Boy or whatever he was gave Sam the creeps. Clenching his jaw, he forced himself to look away.

He went back to his owl pellet as if nothing had happened, picking out the needle-thin bones. Every time he stole a glance out the window, he saw One-Eye, still staring and twitching his tail, but pretended not to notice.

He forced himself to think about Pa and his stories. He loved the one about the time Pa had discovered a dinosaur bone behind an old gas station, and he'd had to fight off a skunk and three vicious raccoons to claim it. Turns out, the bone belonged to a steer, not a dinosaur, but that didn't make the battle any less epic.

Pa had fought off about a zillion wild critters in his day, like the escaped warthog he'd wrestled into submission his first week in the bayou and the pet parrot he'd let free, only to get pooped on as a thank-you.

Drifting back into Pa's stories carried Sam all the way to the lunch bell. As it sounded, an ache sprouted in his stomach at the sudden thought that he might never hear Pa tell them again. That he might never find out for certain which parts were real and which were made up. The truth hadn't seemed so important when Pa was still alive, but now . . .

He needed to see Pa. Too bad he had to wait till after school.

At lunch he got in line like everybody else, even though

119

he could see the lunch ladies talking about him, probably wondering if he was going to freak out and leave his food like yesterday. He smiled when Edie came to join him in line. More than ever, he needed a distraction.

"There's nothing like owl barf right before lunch," she said.

"Yeah. I hope they're not serving dead rodent."

"Nope, just meat loaf."

"Great. I'm not sure which is worse."

"I am." Edie made a queasy face and pointed to a huge metal tray of what looked like dog food.

Sam paid for his meat loaf. Aunt Jo had given him lunch money that morning, even after he said he didn't need it. According to her, lunch was her responsibility now, and he'd decided to keep his mouth shut and not argue.

"Aren't you going to eat?" Sam said, when Edie left without getting a tray.

"No. Barf pellets, remember?"

"Oh, right." They went back to their same spot in the courtyard. It was pretty packed, thanks to the perfect weather. "Hey, you didn't eat yesterday either," Sam realized as he sat down and balanced the plastic tray on his knees.

"Barf is kind of a theme in our cafeteria."

Sam stared down at his meat loaf. "You want some?"

Edie made another face, but she took his corn bread after he told her he thought corn bread tasted like butter-coated sawdust, which it did.

While they ate, Edie told him about the science fair coming up at the community center, and she made it sound like it was going to be awesome and not a grape-soda rainstorm like the one at his old school.

"Are you going to enter your glider?"

Some of the excitement drained from Edie's eyes. "I was, but it costs $50 to enter because they need money to recover from last year's storms, and Mom doesn't have it."

"That stinks."

"Yeah."

"What if you offer to pay her back?"

Edie shook her head and stared down at Sam's barfy meat loaf. "It's okay. I probably wouldn't win anyway. But a lot of people from school are entering."

"What about the money Aunt Jo gave you?"

Edie took her time wiping the corn-bread crumbs off her tights. "I spent it. They were going to shut off the water in our house, so I paid the bill. It was kind of all I had."

"Oh, that double stinks."

"Pretty much."

Sam swallowed another forkful of meat loaf and then wished he hadn't. He bit down on a piece of grit the size of a tooth. He spit the whole bite into his napkin.

"Gross."

"Told you," Edie said.

"Hey, I know. Why don't we enter together? As a team."

"As a team?"

"Yeah, why not?"

Edie thought it over. "But who will pay our entry fee? I told you, I don't have any money."

"I will. I have money from helping Pa clean out the shed and collect worms and stuff."

"I don't want to waste your worm money."

She looked serious, but Sam thought he saw the hint of a smile. "It wouldn't be a waste," he said. "We'd be a team."

"Are you sure?"

"Of course I am."

Now Edie really did smile, and so Sam spent the next few seconds staring down at his shoelaces.

"This is going to be great," Edie said after a while, her eyes sparkling behind her purple glasses. "We can build a brand-new glider and paint it just like your plane, and we can add more solar panels so it'll fly longer. Mr. Redding lets us borrow his panels so we don't have to buy them or anything. Ooh, let's work on it after school. Can you ask Miss J if you can stay late tonight?"

"Sure, but I thought you were sleeping at our house?"

"No, I'd better not. In case Mom comes back."

"Oh, okay."

"So, what do you say?"

Sam thought it over. He didn't want to lie to Edie too, but he already had someplace he needed to be after school. Then again, if he told Aunt Jo he was staying late to work with Edie, she wouldn't have any reason to come looking for him.

"Sounds like a plan."

"Yes!" Edie attempted a high five, but missed and accidentally touched his meat loaf.

"Barf. I'm going inside to wash this off. See you in class."

"Sure."

Once she was gone, he turned around to face the bushes growing all along the edges of the courtyard. "You can come out now."

One-Eye sidled free from the thicket and sniffed at Sam's meat loaf, wrinkling his nose. He tried to rub his bony body against Sam's side, but Sam jerked away.

"Why do you keep following me? Why can't you just leave me and Pa alone?"

A kid sitting nearby looked over as One-Eye slid back into the shadows. Sam didn't say anything else, since now that weird kid was staring, but he could feel One-Eye hiding deep inside the tangle of branches, watching him.

Sam went to the office to call Aunt Jo before the end of lunch. She was just as excited about the science fair as Edie and said she'd try to bring the check when she picked them up. Sam didn't tell her that Edie planned to stay at her own house, or that she didn't need to pay. Maybe he was being a blue jay, but maybe he still didn't like the idea of giving away Pa's money, not when it was one of the only things he had that Pa had actually touched. He definitely didn't tell her where he'd really be after school, though she'd probably find out soon enough.

The rest of the day went faster than he'd expected. Before he knew it, the bell rang. 3:40 p.m. Edie hurried over to his desk.

"I thought we'd design the wings first. Mr. Redding has this software on his computer that's super cool and lets you model for wind speed and resistance and everything. Then we can print the parts out on the 3D printer, except that will probably take all night, so we can't actually see the finished product till the morning."

She said all that without even taking a breath, and Sam was starting to feel extra bad for ditching her. "Okay, I just have to go to the bathroom first."

"Oh yeah, good idea. That way we won't be interrupted."

Edie rushed off to the girls' bathroom, and it was just Sam and Mr. Redding.

"You did nice work today," Mr. Redding said. Sam prepared himself for the big speech about yesterday, but it never came. "Keep it up. You ever use a 3D printer before?"

"No, sir."

"I think you'll like it. We might even be able to repair that plane of yours, if you're willing to put in some extra work."

"Sure." He kept his eyes pinned on his shoelaces, in case Mr. Redding could tell he was lying. 3:41, time to go.

"I can show you how the design software works if you're ready."

"I just need to stop by the bathroom."

Mr. Redding studied him for a moment. His eyes kind of reminded Sam of the Colonel's, the way they seemed to see straight through your skin to the pink stuff hiding underneath.

"I'll only be a minute."

Mr. Redding didn't say anything until Sam was all the way to the door.

"I'll be waiting."

Great.

Sam hid inside the bathroom until he was sure that Edie had come and gone. Then he slipped out and headed straight for the back door so he wouldn't have to go past Mr. Redding's room. The door had one of those red exit signs above it, and he was afraid some kind of alarm would go off, but nothing happened. He walked out into the sun and let the door slam behind him.

He saw the dragonflies before he saw the tree. Some

younger kids were chasing a stream of them across the field behind the school, laughing and trying to jump high enough to touch one. He climbed the hill, blinking at the sea of grass that shivered with thousands of dragonfly wings. There were even more than the day before. As he approached the tree, he saw that the trunk had come to life, rolling in gentle waves of green and blue.

No one had followed him. They probably didn't even realize he was gone. With a deep breath, he stuck his head slowly into the hollow. Sure enough, the inside opened up into a tunnel, just like the day before. He took one last look at the field, pleased to find no sign of One-Eye, then he threw one leg over the lip of the hollow and inhaled the deep, muggy scent of Bayou St. George. The fall wasn't as bad today, now that he was ready for it. He dove forward, and it was kind of like hurtling down the world's strangest slide. Vines and twigs and leaves flitted past. Already he could hear the cicadas humming in the treetops and the bullfrogs rumbling away in their hidden pools, and his heart squeezed in his chest.

A few seconds later, he dropped out on the other side, and the swamp was just the way he'd left it. A giant grasshopper hopped onto his jeans and clung there for a moment before leaping skyward. A cottonmouth with glowing amber eyes and pitch-black scales wrapped around the base of a nearby tupelo. It hissed something that sounded like,

"Nice to see you," and Sam would have laughed if he hadn't been so scared.

Pa used to tell him this funny story about a talking snake, and now Sam was wondering if maybe Pa had been telling the truth all along. A scratching sound drew his attention. Sam's heart seized in his chest as he turned to see One-Eye sitting in the crook of a nearby tree, glaring at him.

"I told you to stay away," Sam said.

One-Eye tilted his head, as if to say *try and make me*, and then suddenly he wasn't the cat anymore, but the Boy.

"But I've got so much more to show you." The Boy jumped down from the tree, landing on all fours like a cat. Then he straightened up and reached out his hand. "I'm here to take you on a little trip down memory lane. You've been wondering, haven't you? If all of those stories your pa told were actually true?"

He had been wondering, but why should he trust the Boy to show him?

"Get out of my way." Sam stalked past, ramming his shoulder into the Boy with satisfying force. But the Boy was quick. He caught Sam by surprise, jabbing him with cold fists, and Sam splatted face-first into a mud puddle. Righting himself, he spun around, cussing, only to find the Boy leaning against a tree, flashing his cruel grin.

"First stop's through here." He pointed toward a particularly shadowy patch of tupelo trees. "Stay here if you like.

Only, I thought you wanted the truth."

The Boy winked before darting off deeper into the forest. As soon as he was gone, the trees on Sam's other side exploded. Branches whipping and cracking, like some mighty beast was beating its way toward him through the brush.

THE BEAST TURNED OUT TO be Pa, a younger version at least, running half-naked through the woods like his life depended on it.

"Pa, wait!" Sam shot up, waving his arms, trying to make sense of what was happening. Before he'd gone two steps, another shape burst through the trees and knocked him back down again. It looked kind of like a rhino, only smaller and twice as fierce.

No way.

It couldn't be.

It was!

The warthog used his tusks to rip through vines and thick leaves, tunneling through the trees like the world's ugliest jackhammer. And he was headed straight for Pa.

"Hey! Leave him alone!" Sam leaped to his feet, splattering mud, and chased after the unlikely duo. Except they weren't unlikely at all. Sam knew this story. Pa had told him a million times about chasing down a warthog that had escaped from the zoo his first week in Louisiana. Had the

Boy been telling the truth? Was he really seeing Pa's memory brought to life?

Sam surged ahead, determined to catch up. Luckily for him, the warthog had cleared a path, so all he had to do was follow. Unluckily for him, he hadn't made the swamp any less treacherous. Twice, he nearly sank in deep holes disguised as mud puddles, and once he had to leap over a cottonmouth as it aimed its poisonous fangs at his ankles.

Sam heard a grunt, followed by a scream. "Pa!"

He broke through into a clearing and there was Pa, as a young man, wrestling a giant warthog, just like in his stories. And like in the stories, the warthog jeered and bucked and made sweeping jabs at the air with his jagged tusks. For his part, Pa looked like a mud wrestler, bobbing and weaving, searching for the perfect angle of attack.

Sam knew he should help, but he just stood there, stunned. It shouldn't have been possible, but here he was, in Pa's memory, and the story of the warthog hadn't been made up after all. It had really happened.

"Time to go." A firm hand closed on Sam's shoulder, and he shrank away at the sight of the Boy, grinning down at him.

"No way. I have to see what happens."

The warthog bucked, sending Pa sprawling. Sam knew it was just a memory, but he couldn't stand by any longer while Pa got pummeled. "Get off me!"

Sam kicked the Boy hard in the shins. The Boy snarled, revealing his tiny, sharp teeth, but Sam was already off, running toward the clearing. He was tearing his way through a tangle of vines when Pa got to his feet again and, somehow, managed to wrap his arms around the warthog's belly. That was when Sam saw something else wrapped around the beast's middle, cutting into his lizardlike skin. That's right! He had almost forgotten how the story ended. It was a coil of barbed wire, and without hesitation, Pa unwrapped it, careful to avoid the flailing tusks. As soon as he did, that wild warthog went quiet as a baby.

The story had been true all along. Did that mean Pa's other stories were true too?

In the moment of quiet that followed, Sam's boot cracked a branch, and Pa turned, a look of surprise registering on his muddy features. Sam opened his mouth to say hello, and then the Boy's hand clamped down on his shoulder once again, cold fingers squeezing tight. The next thing Sam knew, he was being dragged across the treetops like a fish on the end of the world's biggest hook.

He didn't know where the hook was taking him, or why, or how the Boy could change shape and fly, but soon the trees gave way to a twisting black tunnel, streaked with blinking lights that looked an awful lot like stars. The swampy air was replaced by a chilly wind that whistled in his ears and speckled his cheeks with frost. He landed, face-first, in a pile of snow at the edge of a heavily forested mountain. Nearby, a cozy cabin provided the only hint of light.

As he turned over onto his back, a gold streak shot across the sky, followed by another and another. It took him a moment to figure out what they were, since he'd never actually seen one before. Shooting stars!

The back of Sam's neck prickled, and it wasn't from the cold. Pa had only talked about shooting stars once before, when he told the story of how Sam was born. According to Pa, there'd been a whole shower of stars flying across the sky that night, kind of like what was happening right now. Sam went stock-still. Was he about to see himself as a baby? More important, was he about to meet Mama face-to-face?

Pushing against the snowdrifts, he made his way toward the cabin, soon joining up with another set of footprints that led to a round green door. Instead of going in, he ducked beneath the window and peeked through the frosted glass. He glimpsed a crackling fire, the flames painting orange and red streaks on the rustic stone floor. He cleared away some of the frost, so he could see more details of the room inside. There was a threadbare rug in front of the fire, an old rocking chair, a pile of logs, an open suitcase with a familiar broken latch.

A scream interrupted his investigation.

The scream pierced the still night air, and Sam stumbled

back. He knew, without knowing how he knew, that the scream was coming from Mama. It came again, louder this time, and Sam pressed his face to the cracked glass.

He searched the room, fighting against the glare from the fire, and finally, off to his left, he spotted someone. It was Pa! Not much younger than Sam remembered him, kneeling beside a bed, holding a bloody bundle in his arms. Sam stopped breathing, and in that same instant the wind died down, and the sound of Pa's voice doubled the ache twisting in his belly.

"Hang on, now. Keep breathing. Just like that. Don't stop." He watched Pa form a cradle out of blankets and place the red-faced baby inside, kicking and wailing before the fire. It was a little like the story Pa had told of his birth, but not exactly. Pa had always said he was born beneath a sea of shooting stars and that he'd come out bigger than a giant catfish and twice as slippery. From what he could tell, he didn't look all that big, but he definitely looked slippery. Also, he'd never said anything about all that screaming.

As Pa moved aside, he saw her. Mama.

She cried out again, thrashing against the blankets, hands gripping her stomach, and Pa rushed back to her side. He dipped a cloth in water and wiped her forehead, and held her hand, and when he pushed the hair out of her face Sam could see that it was really Mama. He didn't remember seeing her in real life, but he knew her face from the one

133

picture he'd found hidden in Pa's closet. Her curly black hair that billowed out around her head, like an invisible wind was lifting it up from underneath. Her sad brown eyes that made him think of a mountain love song, the kind that always had a tragic end. He pressed his hand to the glass, longing to touch her, but then his world split open.

She threw back her head, screaming yet again. But this scream was different from the others, and she curled up in pain, and he could see the fear on Pa's face . . . No. This couldn't be happening. Sam knew she'd died when he was a boy. A boy. Pa had never said anything about her dying when he was a baby. As much as Pa loved stories, he'd never wanted to talk about this one much, or about Mama. All Sam knew was the part about shooting stars and him being a fat baby, but what if . . . ? What if there was a reason Pa hadn't wanted to tell him? No, this couldn't be happening.

It wouldn't.

Not if he could help it.

He raced around to the front of the cabin and threw open the door. Pa shot up and their eyes met, but then he marched right past Sam like he didn't see him and slammed the door shut. "It's this dang storm," Pa said to Mama, still ignoring Sam. He made sure to lock the door tight this time, and he piled more fresh blankets on top of Mama. "You stay here," Pa said, his face dripping sweat despite the cold. "I'm going to get help."

134

"It's too dangerous," Mama said, and her voice was weak and raw and beautiful. Sam had never heard it before. He walked right up to the bed, shaking, and took Mama's hand. Except he didn't. His hand slipped right through, like maybe he was the ghost and not the other way around.

"Mama?" Sam said. She didn't respond. She didn't even look at him. It was like before in the forest when Pa had run right past him. Sam thought he'd just been distracted by the warthog, but maybe part of being in Pa's memory was that he wasn't really here, at least not where anyone could see him.

He reached out again as Mama moaned, every inch of him longing to touch her, to comfort her, but all he could do was watch.

Pa picked up the baby, blankets and all, and settled it in Mama's arms. Sam had to admit that he was a fat baby, but not nearly as big as a giant catfish. "I'll be back before you know it."

He stood to go, but Mama caught his hand. "Not this time, Jack West. You're staying right here with me. You and I both know there's no one around for at least fifty miles and no car and no one else fool enough to be out in this storm. So you'll stay right here where you belong, and you'll promise me something."

Slowly, like it was taking the weight of the world to drag him down, Pa sank into the mattress beside Mama.

"He ain't yours, and so I don't blame you if you can't, but—" Mama let out a deep cough and grasped her belly. Pa reached for the water, but she drew him back. "Promise me you'll be his daddy. I know it's a lot, and maybe I don't have the right to ask, but there it is. You're a good man, Jack West, and I'm asking."

The firelight painted lines down Pa's face, making him look older than he really was. "But he is mine, Little Mama. I told you that the first day we met. Remember? There you were, just about pregnant as can be, wrestling a rattlesnake with your bare hands. I've seen a lot of wild sights in my life, and I've done a lot of wild things myself, but nothing quite like that. Now, you look at this boy here and tell me he's not a West."

Mama smiled, and she cried a little, too, and then she doubled up and screamed. The sound cut right into Sam's chest, and he reached for her hand again, but it was too late. Just as Mama went still, her body giving one final, quiet shudder, the invisible hook snagged Sam behind the belly button, and he was flying.

He fought and kicked and grabbed at the air, but nothing he did could stop it. "No! Let go!" he cried. He had to get back. He had to save Mama, to make her see him. To say he was sorry for being the reason she was dead. But he kept on flying.

No wonder Pa had never told him the full story.

He had known Pa wasn't his real dad, not in the technical sense, but he'd never known the truth about Mama's death. How could Pa have kept it from him? Why had he spent so much time telling him stories about ghost lights and mermaids, but he'd never once mentioned that Mama had wrestled rattlesnakes? Or that she'd died because of him?

Thoughts racing, he dropped out of the sky and slammed onto solid ground. He expected to be back in Holler, staring up at the ugly yellow sun, but he wasn't.

His fingers touched the damp wood of the dock behind the little white house, his house, and he could hear water burbling calmly down below. Everything was so quiet and serene. Almost like nothing had happened, but it had. Because now he knew that Pa's stories were real, but he also knew that Pa had lied about Mama. Someone whistled nearby, and Sam spun around to find the Boy perched atop the same post, tapping the face of his watch.

"You're running out of time, young man. Tick-tock and all that."

Already the sun was dropping behind the trees, coloring the canopy a deep rustic amber. But it was too soon. Yesterday, he'd spent an entire afternoon with Pa, but today . . . all he'd done was chase shadows. He needed more time. He needed to ask Pa why he'd never told him about—

"Sam, you're back." Pa came out of the house, the screen

door banging shut behind him, and he scooped Sam into his arms. "I've been waiting. I was starting to think that yesterday was all a dream."

"I thought the same thing," Sam said, and he pressed his face into Pa's shirt and breathed in the scent of sweat and raw fish and motor oil. When Pa finally let him go, he was relieved to see that it was his pa, the one he remembered, not some younger version who couldn't see him. Pa's gaze drifted over Sam's shoulder, and he turned, expecting to see the Boy, but the Boy was gone. Instead, he saw the canoe bobbing in the water, knocking gently against the dock like it was waiting for them to climb in.

That got Sam thinking. True, he wanted to ask about Mama and everything that had happened on that cold, awful night, but all that could wait. The canoe had given him an idea, at least the start of one. Why hadn't he thought of it before? If the Boy was right, and the doorway would close up before long, then there was only one solution. He had to bring Pa back with him—before that happened.

He wanted to kick himself. He'd wasted so much time lately thinking about how Pa would never be able to eat his favorite pizza again or track down the Colonel, when really he should have been finding a way to get Pa back.

"Come on. We have to go." Sam climbed into the boat and waited for Pa to follow.

"Go where?" he said. A few feet away, a pair of milky

138

yellow eyes surfaced, a massive snakelike shadow darkening the water. Sam knew it was the Colonel. Pa saw him, too, but he didn't look worried. Sam had a feeling there was more to Pa's relationship with the Colonel than he'd let on.

"Please, we have to hurry. I'm going to take you back."

At those words, Pa seized Sam's hand and hopped into the boat. Green water splashed over the sides, but not enough to slow them down. Like before, the canoe moved of its own accord, and the Colonel followed them, his massive body leaving a wide wake just beneath the surface. And below him, illuminated in the strangely glowing water, Sam thought he could make out other shapes: catfish the size of sharks, pale yellow lights bobbing against the current, purple tendrils dancing in the depths, and a sparkling pink tailfin that could only belong to one of Pa's imaginary mermaids.

Sam stared in wonder as the canoe cut a steady path across the surface.

As they approached the far bank, he turned to Pa. "I saw Ma today." He tried hard not to let the ache in his belly show on his face. "You never told me she wrestled a rattle-snake."

Pa laughed, and Sam explained some more about the memories and the Boy who looked like Pa, or a cat, but wasn't either. He didn't say anything about it being his fault that Ma had died. He figured he'd save that conversation for later, once he had Pa back safe and sound. They agreed, in those few seconds drifting toward shore, to make the Boy their enemy. Because what else could you call someone who tried to keep the two of them apart?

"Now!"

As soon as they hit the shore, they ran. Sam could already feel the tug starting up in his belly, and he knew that any second now he'd be dragged away and the hollow would be closed up tight until tomorrow. Fine. Let the Boy drag him—but this time he wouldn't go alone.

Sam squeezed Pa's hand, and they pounded their way through mud and weeds to the tree.

"You first!" he cried, but it was too late. Before Pa could move an inch, the world turned into one ginormous tornado. A force greater than any he'd felt so far ripped him free from Pa's grasp, and he was hurtling into the hollow. He tried to grab on, to stop himself, to scream, but the tunnel zipped by at frightening speed, going up and up and up, leaves and twigs tearing at his skin, and no matter how hard he fought, he kept right on flying.

10

HE HIT THE GROUND WITH an almighty crack, and for a second he was certain he was dead and gone, just like Pa. Slowly, Sam rolled onto his back blinking up at the sun. A sudden gust of air ruffled his hair, and he sat up just as a stream of glittering blue and green disappeared inside the hollow. A group of kids ran after it, laughing and reaching their hands into the tree, pulling out clumps of dirt and dead leaves.

"I don't understand. Where'd they all go?" one of the kids said.

"Stop that!" Sam said, dragging himself to his feet. "Get out of here!"

At the sight of Sam shouting and waving his arms, the kids raced back to the baby playground, squealing with laughter.

Sam ignored them. He didn't have time for games. He thrust his hand into the hollow, and then his head, ignoring how the rough bark scraped at his skin. He punched and clawed at the wood, but it was no use. He'd failed.

With that thought slicing through his brain, he sank to the ground again, defeated.

The wind lifted his hair and rattled the few dead leaves still clinging to the tree. He'd left Pa behind, but he wouldn't make the same mistake tomorrow. All he had to do was act fast, get the Boy or the cat or whatever out of the way, and then he and Pa could escape before time ran out.

A surge of hope like he hadn't felt in weeks filled his chest. *But what if it doesn't work and the doorway closes for good?* that same cruel voice whispered in his head. Then he'd just have to make sure that he and Pa couldn't get separated. Use a rope, or maybe handcuffs. When the invisible hook came to get him, it would capture Pa, too, and then they'd both be sucked out the other side.

His brain whirring with plans, Sam got to his feet, surprised to find he wasn't hurt. It all seemed so simple now. Pa might be dead, but that didn't mean he had to stay that way. Sam could bring him back.

"Hey, there you are." Edie jogged over, her purple hair blowing wild around her head. "What are you doing out here?"

"Nothing. I just . . . I needed some air." Sam didn't like lying to Edie, but he was a lot more concerned with his plan.

"Are you okay?" She tugged on the sleeves of her flannel. It was the same one she'd worn the day before, since she hadn't gone home to change. She cocked her head. "Is it about your dad?"

"No. Well, yes, but . . . you wouldn't understand."

Edie's expression hardened, her mouth straightening into a thin line. "I lost my dad too, remember?"

"I know, but this is different."

He could feel the hurt simmering behind Edie's eyes, but he didn't know what to say to make it better, and he didn't have time to focus on someone else's problems.

"You're right, it is different," she said, and he couldn't tell if she was mad at him or just sad about her dad leaving.

Sam wiped the dirt off his pants, trying to think of something to say. He didn't want to hurt Edie's feelings, but he couldn't tell her about the tree or Pa or any of it.

"I'm sorry. Forget about it," she said. He watched the anger drain out of Edie's face, and she leaned in close to him. For a wild moment, he thought she was going to kiss him, which sent his already chaotic thoughts into a frenzy, but instead she plucked a piece of bark from his hair. "What were you doing out here anyway? I was waiting for almost an hour."

Sam's throat had gone dry, and he racked his brain for an answer, a lie, anything.

"Mr. Redding had to go home. He looked pretty upset. And I had to wait in the office with Miss Ross." She crinkled up her lips like she'd just eaten a bad lemon. Whoever

Miss Ross was, Edie clearly wasn't a fan. "Anyway, I already called Miss J to pick us up. Are you sure you're all right?"

"I'm fine. I guess I lost track of time."

She frowned, giving him that same sad–puppy-dog look all his neighbors had worn on the day of Pa's funeral. "It's okay. We can work on the project this weekend. As long as you promise not to disappear on me again." Edie held out her pinkie. "Swear on it?"

"Sure." A lump caught in Sam's throat as they inter-locked pinkies. Tomorrow was the day he would rescue Pa, for real this time, no two ways about it. He didn't have time to think about some science fair project, but he also didn't want to hurt Edie's feelings. "Sounds like fun."

Baby Girl crunched over the hill just as Sam and Edie released their pinkies. Sam climbed into the back so Edie could have the front seat, but she scooted in beside him.

"Do I look like a chauffeur?" Aunt Jo said, but she laughed and pumped the gas anyway, bumping away toward home. Her home, at least, but it would never be Sam's, not really.

"You can take me to my house, Miss J," Edie said over the twangy bluegrass music blaring from the radio. Pa would have approved. "Mom's sister called and said she's coming home early, and I've got dishes and laundry and stuff."

"We'll see." Aunt Jo's reflection in the rearview mirror turned grim. "And you can bet I'm gonna have a talk with your mama when she gets back."

Edie gave Sam a worried look. As they approached Edie's house, which was just down the street from Aunt Jo's, Sam saw lights on inside and a beat-up hatchback with about a hundred bumper stickers parked crooked in the driveway.

"See, I told you she'd be home." Edie jumped out. When Aunt Jo started to follow, she blocked her door. "Maybe you can just give her a day to settle in and then talk to her. She's trying her best."

"She needs to try harder. She should be taking care of you, not the other way around." Sam couldn't understand why Aunt Jo sounded so angry, but then her tone softened. "You call me if you need anything. Anything, you hear?"

"Yes, Miss J."

Edie lingered on the curb a few seconds longer.

"See you later?" Sam said, because as usual he couldn't think of anything really good to say.

"Definitely. Oh, if it's okay, Sam and I are going to work on our project this weekend."

"Sure thing, just call me and I'll pick you up. How'd it go today by the way? Ready to launch into space yet?"

Edie looked at Sam and then back at Aunt Jo. "Not just yet, but it went great. We're almost done designing the wings."

"Right on. Nice to see you two working as a team. I can't wait to see it when it's finished."

"Bye." Edie offered a weak wave. When Aunt Jo wasn't

looking, she winked at Sam, which made his cheeks heat up and his insides squirm.

Aunt Jo didn't drive away until Edie had gone inside, and even then she was muttering.

"Is she . . . ?" Sam started, and then realized he didn't know the right way to finish. "I mean, Edie's mom, is she—?"

"An addict? Like me?" Aunt Jo shot him a look in the rearview mirror. "You bet your socks she is. The longest she ever had was two months clean, and that was over a year ago. Thought she might make it this time, but you know how it is with addicts."

Sam didn't know how it was. He still thought of addicts as the people you saw huddled on street corners, not his friend's mom. Not Aunt Jo. She reached over and turned the music all the way down. "It's like having a disease. Just when you think you've kicked it, it rears its ugly head again. It was like that for me, too, when I first got back."

"Got back from where?"

"Afghanistan. I'd lost my leg and my career. They wanted to park me behind a desk, but I've never been any good at sitting around. I got angry. I lost myself."

Silence settled over the car as Aunt Jo pulled up the driveway in front of the big yellow house. The huge maples on either side cast the car in shadow.

"Is that why you couldn't call or write? Because you lost yourself?"

She turned back to face him, her expression not angry or sad, just quiet, resigned. After a pause, she spoke. "You know, even though I was taller and tougher than your pa, I always looked up to him. I don't know, maybe it's bound to be that way with older brothers. Everything I did—flight school, my service—it was for me, sure, but it was also for him. Pops never understood why I wanted to go into something he considered 'man's work,' but your pa didn't bat an eye. He always stood up for me when Pops took one of his stands on old-fashioned values. I guess that's why your pa's opinion mattered most. I always wanted to make him proud."

Aunt Jo paused and all Sam could hear was the sound of her breathing. "At first, I thought I could keep it from him, pretend like nothing was wrong. I don't think I believed there was anything wrong myself. All I was doing was taking medication the doctor had prescribed, and I needed it for the pain, and I mean really needed it. You try losing half a leg and not taking any pills. The problem was that, even after the worst of the physical pain went away, I couldn't stop."

Her hands gripped and released the steering wheel, worn hands with wrinkled knuckles, just like Pa's. "I drove down for your ninth birthday. I bet you didn't know that." She turned around to face the back but didn't meet Sam's eyes. "I thought I was fine, normal, but on the way there, I drove off the road. Just like that. One second I was moving along the curves, same as always, the next I was off in a ditch, wheels spinning, my whole world turned upside down."

Sam heard the words but it took them a while to register. "You had an accident?" Images of Pa's Sunbird flashed through his head, but he forced them back down again.

"Nearly died. Somehow, my phone didn't break, and I called your pa before I even called 911. He was the one who pulled me out." She rested her forehead on her hands for a moment and closed her eyes. "He didn't know about the pills until we got to the hospital."

"No. He would have told me. He said you couldn't make it because you had some army reunion." And it was too weird. Two accidents in one family. Three, if you counted what had happened to One-Eye.

"That's because I asked him to."

"You're lying. He would have told me if you'd had an accident. No way he wouldn't."

She didn't say anything for a long while. It got so hot inside the car that Sam cracked the door to let in some air. "Do you know why I drove down that day?"

"It was my birthday. You always come down. You always came down."

148

"And what did we always do on your birthday?"

"I don't know, birthday stuff. We had cake and you drove me to the aviation museum and . . . oh."

"Yeah, oh. If things had been different, just a little, then you might have been with me in that car when I crashed."

"But I wasn't." Suddenly, the air was closing in around him.

"But you could have been."

The clouds shifted and a slant of sunlight flooded the car. Sweat dripped down Sam's back, but he ignored it.

"Come on," Aunt Jo said. "Let's go inside."

"No, wait." He pushed past the images of twisted metal still swirling in his head and tried hard to focus. "What did you mean earlier when you said that Pa asked you to stay away?"

Aunt Jo turned to the back seat and this time she did meet his eyes. "I was mad about it at first, but I don't blame your pa. He was only trying to protect you."

"Oh." Protect him? By sending Aunt Jo away for four years? He couldn't stand the idea of Pa ignoring his own sister, all because of one tiny mistake. All because of him. With everything that was happening, and with all he'd learned about Ma, he was beginning to wonder if he'd ever known Pa at all.

She opened the door and a wave of hot air flooded the car.

149

"You could have told me." Sam's words hung in the space between them. "You could have called."

Aunt Jo sighed but didn't answer right away. "Recovery is tough, and I wasn't always doing as well as I am now. I wanted to protect you too, like your pa, but maybe . . . I don't know, maybe I was really protecting myself."

Sam didn't know what to say to that. After a while, Aunt Jo shut her door and popped the trunk. "Hey, I thought we'd make something special for dinner," she said, trying to sound cheery. "Picked up the ingredients today at work." Aunt Jo worked part-time at the grocery store and part-time fixing cars out of her garage.

Sam got out and stretched his legs. He hadn't noticed it before, but they did feel a little stiff and bruised from where he'd been dragged down the tunnel.

"Here, you take these two." She hoisted two heavy paper sacks into his arms. "Got everything we need for your pa's special turkey-and-bacon lasagna. What do you say, think you can help me make it?"

Sam shrugged. He wasn't mad at Aunt Jo like he'd been when he first arrived, but that didn't mean he was ready to be best friends either.

"Well, I sure hope you can help me eat it, because I'm trying to lose weight, Bucko, not chow down on an entire lasagna by myself."

Inside, Aunt Jo cranked up some Clifton Chenier and His Red Hot Louisiana Band. That was Pa's favorite CD of all time, and Sam wondered where she'd gotten it. Then he wondered if maybe it wasn't her CD at all, but Pa's.

"How about you slice up these onions?"

Sam didn't know how he felt about Aunt Jo maybe stealing Pa's CD, but he started chopping. It was nice listening to the familiar, bluesy tunes. He didn't even mind the onions burning his eyes or the way Aunt Jo chopped the bacon into chunks instead of slices like Pa always did. Once the bacon and onions started frying and the turkey started sizzling, Aunt Jo's ugly old house even smelled a little bit like home.

While they waited for the turkey to finish, Sam sat down at the kitchen table. Aunt Jo brought him a tall glass of sweet tea, which wasn't Orange Crush, but was still pretty good.

"You know, I talked to your pa the day of the accident. Before it happened, I mean." Aunt Jo released a huge sigh as she sat down. She had bacon grease on her shirt and a piece of onion skin stuck to her sleeve.

"On my birthday?"

"No, not my accident, your pa's." She fumbled with the chip hanging from her neck, digging her fingernails into the grooves. "That bothered me a lot at first, me surviving an accident and your pa . . . well, if one of us deserved to

151

die, it sure as heck wasn't him."

Sam swallowed, letting the words sink in. "What'd he say? Was he . . . ?"

"He talked about you—what else?" Aunt Jo smiled, sitting up straight again and returning to her usual, no-nonsense self.

Sam wished he could do the same. Instead, something hard settled into the back of his throat.

"Said how you'd caught a catfish as thick as a mailbox, and how you'd probably make it into *Bobby Joe's Catch of the Week* a second time, which was a record for someone your age. He said how you were doing well in school, and how you'd nearly won the hundred meters in track and how he wanted me to come down again to visit." She paused, picking the onion peel from her sleeve. "That was the real reason he called. He . . ."

Sam waited. Aunt Jo got that look on her face like her cheeks hurt and maybe her eyes too, on the inside not the outside, and Sam knew just how she felt because his face didn't feel all that great either. An ache sprouted behind his eyes and filled up his throat, and suddenly he couldn't listen to Clifton Chenier or smell Pa's lasagna or look at Aunt Jo's face for one more single second. True, he would get Pa back soon enough, but what if? What if he didn't?

"I need to go upstairs." He stood and then he waited for

a second, thinking maybe he would change his mind, but he didn't, and so he went upstairs and Aunt Jo didn't stop him.

Safe in his room, he closed the door and buried his face in his cat-hair pillow. He tried not to think about what would happen if he failed. If the doorway closed and Pa got stuck over there, and he got stuck over here, and he had nothing left of Pa but a stolen CD, a bunch of old stories, and a dish full of not-quite-Pa's lasagna.

11

LATER THAT EVENING, SAM WOKE up to a gentle knocking and the sound of retreating footsteps. He could tell before he even opened the door that Aunt Jo was holding another one of her meetings. Friendly voices filtered up the stairs, along with the patter of clinking silverware. Sam wondered if Edie was in the kitchen again serving cake.

Part of him wanted to go down and check, but then he found the cardboard file box sitting outside his door. On top was a plate wrapped in tin foil and a note:

Hope the lasagna turned out all right :)
P.S. These are some of your pa's things. I thought you should have them.

Sam pulled the box into his room and sat down on the floor to examine it. On the side, Pa had scribbled in black Sharpie: *Jack's stuff—don't touch!* Sam remembered that box from their garage back home, but he'd never looked inside. Jack. That's what Ma had called him. Sam knew it was Pa's name, but it was still weird seeing it in writing.

Careful not to tip over the lasagna, Sam lifted both the lid and the plate onto the floor and set them aside. The smell of dusty papers filled his nostrils, settling all around his head like a cloud. He pulled stacks of pictures from crumbling manila envelopes and spread them across the floor. There was Pa when he was still called Jack, wearing those same dirty overalls, all curled up in a ball while One-Eye, the real One-Eye, tried to lick his face. There was Aunt Jo, looking huge and awkward, standing next to a bike that was a few sizes too small. Pa was there too, sitting in the grass with One-Eye cradled in his lap like a baby.

"That cat sure loved your pa." Aunt Jo peeked into the room, and the low hum of voices drifted in from down below. "I think your pa was the only thing he ever did love. Never cared much for me or Pops, and I can't blame him. He was a hard cat to warm up to, but not for Jack."

Sam sifted through more of the photos. One-Eye was in most all of them. "Is it true Pa rescued him after he got hit by a car?"

"Sure is. I guess we Wests have a thing about cars." She shook her head, dropping her gaze. "But I bet your pa told you all about One-Eye. Knowing how much he loves his stories."

"I guess." Sam thought back, thinking how strange it

was that, of all of Pa's stories, he'd chosen to leave this one out. If he'd really loved that ugly cat so much, how come he'd never mentioned him? *And what about Mama?* whispered the nagging voice that kept popping up in his head. "How'd he die?"

Aunt Jo knelt down, every bone in her legs creaking and crunching. "That was the part your pa never could get over. He went to sleep one night, snuggled into a furry ball on your pa's pillow, same as always. Only, the next morning, when Jack went to wake him up, he was already gone. Just like that. After all he'd been through, surviving the accident, scrabbling with raccoons and wild dogs. After all that, your pa couldn't understand why he went to sleep one night and never woke up again."

"What happened?"

"Nobody knows. Sometimes, life isn't fair. One minute you're here and everything's fine, the next minute . . ." Aunt Jo tugged on the poker chip around her neck. It was green, and now, up close, he saw that it said *one year*. "After that, your pa wouldn't talk about One-Eye anymore. He put all his pictures away, except the one by his bed, and if anybody asked, he'd say he'd never had a cat."

Sam's breath had grown heavy in his chest, but he thought he understood. It was the same way he could barely stand to hear stories about Pa. Maybe Pa had wanted to tell him about One-Eye and Mama, only he couldn't find the strength.

Sam wasn't sure how he felt about that, Pa only trusting him with part of the truth.

After a bit, Aunt Jo stood up with a groan. She rubbed down her left leg and Sam found himself wondering for the first time what it had been like. Losing a part of herself that she'd thought would always be there. Waking up one day expecting to find it, for life to be normal, and then remembering all over again that it was gone.

"You'd better eat up," Aunt Jo said, "before your food gets cold." Sam had already forgotten about the lasagna, but now that she mentioned it he could smell the aroma of warm bacon and turkey rising up over all that dust. "Come downstairs if you want. We've got pies tonight. Oh, and I almost forgot." She reached into the pocket of her cargo pants and pulled out a cold Orange Crush. "I had Earl pick up a few cases from the city. They don't sell them at the Shop 'n' Save."

"Thanks." Sam took the can. He had the sudden urge to cry again.

"I should get back. Meeting's about to start. Thank you for . . ." She trailed off. When she found Sam's eyes, she looked like the old Aunt Jo again, like some of her ugly layers had been peeled away and she was more like the person

157

he remembered. "I just . . . I'm glad you're here."

She shut the door and left him holding his can of Orange Crush, the little beads of condensation dripping down his fingertips.

Sam sorted through the photos a while longer. Most of them were from Oklahoma. He could tell by the dried-out grass and open fields, but a few were from the tiny white house in Louisiana. He knew that Pa had moved there after he left home, but he'd never really thought about how strange that was. Pa moving there when he was a kid, and now Sam moving here. Did that mean that Pa had thought of this place as home, at least back then? Had he been missing the dusty gravel roads and the dead fields and the wind that sucked all the liquid from your eyes the minute you stepped out of the car?

Sam found a stack of notebooks hiding under all the pictures. He flipped through a few, surprised to find them filled with Pa's messy writing. Entire notebooks full, some recent, others dating all the way back to when Pa was a boy.

His palms tingled as he turned to a random page, the sound of Pa's voice filling his head.

June 12, 1988

I should've known it was a bad idea to go out gator hunting with Pops and the Earle brothers. This whole trip was doomed from the start, but you know Pops. Head as

158

hard as a boulder and twice as thick. And he wouldn't even let Jojo come with us, which was the biggest blue-jay move of all. She's the one who once shot a coyote from three hundred feet away when it was trying to eat Miss Carla May's dog, and who cares if she's a girl? She's the one who likes hunting and tracking, whereas me, I'm what Pops would call a bona fide wuss, and proud of it.

Now I'm stuck out in Nowheresville, Louisiana, just me and three jerks with guns, trying not to get sucked dry by the world's biggest mosquitoes. Hand to God, I saw one as big as my fist, and don't get me started on the roaches. Good news is, we're heading home in the morning. Bad news is, Pops ain't speaking to me any-more after what went down with the Colonel.

The Colonel? Sam's heart did a flip-flop in his chest. Pa had never told him about heading down to Louisiana with Pops, or about Pops running into the Colonel.

Here's how it went, more or less. The Earle brothers were the first to spot him, this huge, legendary gator, coming out of a cave down in a place called Mermaid Cove. Pops gave the sign, and the boat grew dead quiet. I pulled up the oars while the others aimed their shot-guns. Now, we'd all heard about the Colonel down at the bait shop, and I knew those Earle brothers were itching to make history, not to mention a whole lot of dough. Me, not so much.

I never did have the stomach for hunting. In that awful moment, waiting for the first shot, it was like a hand closed around my throat and I could see how it would all go down. Shots fired, ears ringing, a cloud of blood staining the water. Then the Colonel's body would bob to the surface, and Kit and Marley would be laughing, because that's Kit and Marley for you, and Pops would drag the Colonel out of the water and he'd be just another dead gator. Not a legend, not the oldest gator that ever lived, just some dead piece of meat to be stuffed or sliced up to make wallets.

That's when I shouldered my rifle, the one I'd only ever used for shooting cans, and fired a shot at the clouds. The Colonel started. I swear his yellow eyes met mine, and then he dove into the depths before Kit or Marley or Pops could get off a shot.

On the way home, Pops said that was the last time he'd ever take me hunting, and that I was a disappointment and that he couldn't so much as look me in the face. I said all that was fine by me. If Pops wanted a hunting buddy, he should stop being stubborn and take JoJo, girl or no girl. If not, he should adopt the Earle brothers as his sons and leave me the heck alone.

The only good thing about this trip was the place itself. The swamp. Bayou St. George, they call it. Now, if you subtract Pops and those ornery brothers, it would make a mighty fine place to live. Even accounting for the giant skeeters and roaches. From what I can tell, it's a place chock-full of stories. The kind of place that gets its hooks in you and refuses to let go. Who knows, maybe I'll find my way back there someday. The way Pops and I have been at each other's throats, maybe someday soon.

Sam couldn't believe his eyes. Here was a side of Pa he'd never known before. Sure, he knew how Pa only ever took his camera when they went gator "hunting," and he knew he had a special liking for the Colonel, but he'd never heard about the trip with Pops. It seemed once again that, out of all his stories, Pa had never seen fit to tell Sam the most important ones, like what had really happened to Ma or how he'd first discovered Bayou St. George.

The thought opened up a tiny wound in Sam's chest.

And what about Pa and the Colonel? He thought back once again to how the Colonel had gone after the Boy, almost like he was protecting Sam and Pa. Did the Colonel remember how Pa had helped him all those years ago?

He flipped through another notebook and another, each one older than the last. Pa talked about going to school in Holler, Oklahoma, riding bikes with Aunt Jo. He even found a passage where Pa told the story of letting the possum in the teacher's lounge, and how it'd taken Mr. Redding a whole day to chase it down. That one made him laugh out loud. Especially the part about the possum chomping down on Mr. Redding's mustache.

Mind reeling with new information, he picked up a more recent journal and paged through until the words *Jo* and *birthday* caught his eye.

September 15, 2017

Jo called the house today, asking for Sam. She wanted to wish him happy birthday. I know it's been a year, and she says she's doing better now, but I can't forgive her for what happened. What almost happened. It's like Pops all over again. Jo doesn't remember, because she could only see the good things about Pops, never the bad. She was so desperate for him to notice her, it didn't matter what he did. But he was a mean drunk, and he never cared about anybody but himself.

Like that time he backed into a flagpole outside that old gas station off Route 270. I was five, maybe six, and I conked my head good on the dashboard, but he made me tell Ma I'd tripped and hit a rock. Ma left not long after that. Not that I blamed her. That's a lie. I did blame her, but at least I understood.

That wreck could've been a whole lot worse, the one

162

with Jo, not with Pops. Dang, we sure have a thing with wrecks in this family. And if Sam had been in the car . . . well then, I don't know what I would have done. That's why I can't have her here. Not yet. I said I'd pass on the birthday message, though, but in the end I never did.

Maybe next year, when she's got her life together, things'll be different.

Sam closed the notebook, letting Pa's words settle in. Part of him was angry, because the Pa he knew would never have lied to him. But part of him understood. Pa was trying to protect him.

Strange, how you could know someone so well and not really know them at all.

He wanted to read through all the notebooks, every single page, but he was too tired. Brain tired. And tomorrow was a big day. He ran through his plan one more time in his head. First step, find Pa. No more listening to the creepy boy or running off after warthogs. Next step, tie Pa and him together, so that when the mysterious force came up and yanked him back, Pa would be dragged out right along with him.

Speaking of step two . . . he'd had all day to think of the best way to tether himself to Pa. Rope could work, like the lasso on the wall, but it took a long time to tie a solid knot. He didn't have handcuffs or wire, but he had something even better. Something that had gotten him and Pa out of some truly dire scrapes.

He dug through his stuff, currently sitting in a heap by Pa's dresser, and pulled out a roll of duct tape. It was quick, easy, and nearly indestructible. Pa had once used it to fasten the Sunbird onto the back of his old truck, and he'd towed that car ten miles over some of the bumpiest roads imaginable. If duct tape could hold the Sunbird, then surely it was strong enough for Pa.

After securing the roll in his backpack, Sam finally sat down and took the foil off his plate of lasagna. It was cold, but still tasty. True, the bacon was all chopped up and she'd forgotten to add jalapeños, but it tasted like home, and maybe that wasn't such a bad thing.

He thought about going downstairs to wash his plate and maybe say hi to Edie but decided not to. Instead he took a long shower and brushed his teeth. It felt good to be grit free.

Even though it was still early, he decided his brain needed a rest. It took a long time to fall asleep with so many thoughts battling in his head. Like how maybe Aunt Jo wasn't a stranger after all, and how maybe things would have been different if Pa hadn't asked her to stay away. Then he thought about Pa and the Colonel, and how Pa was waiting for him right now, wondering if this would be the moment Sam returned.

Then other thoughts slipped in. Like how he'd promised

to help Edie with the science fair and how he worried about her mom and about Edie being home all alone and how, sometimes, when he closed his eyes in class, he'd think about her. About the cute way she wore her glasses or how, when she smiled, it lit up her whole face.

But how could he think about Edie when Pa needed his help?

And then he thought how things had changed with Aunt Jo, in the space of only a few days, and how maybe if Holler, Oklahoma, started to feel like home, to really feel like home, then one day he'd forget about Pa altogether. And what then? Then he'd move on and that would mean he'd never really loved Pa in the first place. That would mean that his whole life, everything he and Pa had ever done together, would be a lie.

Except that would never happen. Sam was going to get Pa back.

12

AUNT JO OFFERED TO MAKE eggs for breakfast on Saturday morning, but instead they ate warmed-up turkey lasagna in chipped ceramic mugs.

"We missed you last night," Aunt Jo said. She poured herself a cup of coffee without offering him any. Pa always let Sam sip coffee from his thermos whenever they got up early to fish. It tasted like dirt and burned like lava, but Pa said that's because coffee is an acquired taste. Something you can only learn to love over time.

"Sorry. I guess I fell asleep."

"I figured."

Sam washed the dishes while Aunt Jo finished her coffee. He thought about asking if he could take some leftover lasagna to Edie's place, since that's where they were headed, but then he thought how Aunt Jo might think he liked Edie if he offered to bring her lasagna, as in like-liked her, as in more than just a friend, and it was way too early in the morning for that conversation.

The reason they were going over to Edie's was partly to work on their project, partly to help Edie's mom do stuff around the house, like clean out the gutters and mow the grass, at least according to Aunt Jo. But Sam knew she really wanted to check up on Edie.

"Baby Girl heads out in five." Aunt Jo chugged the last of her coffee and clanked her mug on the counter. "You ready?"

"Hang on. I just need to get something."

Up in his room, he grabbed his backpack, checking to make sure the roll of duct tape was still in the bottom. It seemed kind of weird carrying around a backpack with only one thing inside, so he added a flashlight, a few comics, and an old shirt to even it out.

"One minute to launch," Aunt Jo called from downstairs.

Sam did a quick scan of his room, wishing he had more time to iron out the first part of his plan. He knew what to do once he got inside the tree, but the hard part would be convincing Aunt Jo to drive him there, at the exact right time, and then getting her to leave him alone long enough to rescue Pa. He'd gone over a bunch of possible stories in his head, but each one sounded less believable than the last.

The front door banged shut, and outside he heard Baby Girl's engine revving to life. Great. Time was up. He'd have to wing it.

He raced down the stairs and climbed into Baby Girl just as she started rolling down the driveway. Aunt Jo kept right on driving, despite the fact that his legs were dangling and he couldn't get hold of the door long enough to shut it.

"Cutting it close," Aunt Jo said, braking hard at the end of the drive. Sam seized the opportunity to pull his legs inside and slam the door.

"What was that? You could have run me over."

"Don't blame me, that was Baby Girl. If there's one thing you'll learn fast around here, it's that Baby Girl waits for no one." She gave the dash a loving pat, like Baby Girl was a puppy, not a piece-of-junk car. With that, she pumped the gas and sped off, and Sam couldn't decide if he should be mad or laugh or maybe both.

A few minutes later, they arrived at Edie's house. He hadn't noticed before how different it was from Aunt Jo's. While the outside of Aunt Jo's house looked like an ad from some fancy catalog, Edie's house reminded him of a sad gray turtle, with its squat exterior, sloping roof, and peeling paint. Weeds the size of small horses sprouted from the flowerbeds, creeping up the warped siding and enclosing each of the windows. The hatchback in the driveway was gone, but then he saw that the garage was open and there was Edie coming outside to meet them.

She hurried over at the sight of Baby Girl and tapped on Sam's window.

"Hey," he said, turning the crank as far as it would go.

"Hey." She pulled the sleeves of her purple hoodie tight

around her chest. "Sorry you had to drive all this way. Mom's still sleeping. She wanted me to ask if maybe you could come back tomorrow?" Edie stared down at the curb the whole time she was talking, and Sam had the annoying urge to reach out and touch her hand.

"Asleep at this hour?" Aunt Jo said, shutting off the engine and getting out of the car. "Not if I can help it. You still keep the mower in the shed out back?"

"Actually, I think we're out of gas and most of my science project stuff is still at school, so we should probably—"

"That's why I always come prepared." Sam heard Aunt Jo pop the trunk and decided he'd might as well get out too.

"Sorry," he said to Edie, but not loud enough for Aunt Jo to hear.

"Brought extra gas, a ladder, and a Weedwacker," she said as she set each down on the driveway. She paused for a moment, her face scrunched up in a frown. He wondered if her leg might be hurting her but didn't feel right asking, and then she continued on as if nothing had happened. "Now, why don't you two wheel that mower out here while I go inside and have a talk with your mom."

Edie looked panic-stricken as Aunt Jo stomped off toward the house. Sam wished he could help, but his brain was still a vat of grape soda that could never come up with the right words when he needed them.

Aunt Jo was struggling with the screen door when Edie slumped down farther into her hoodie and followed the stone path up to the house. "She's not here," she said, her voice suddenly flat and hard around the edges.

"Who's not?" Aunt Jo spun around, fire in her eyes, and for a minute Sam was glad he wasn't on the receiving end of her wrath.

Edie didn't answer, and Aunt Jo didn't push it. Instead she gave Edie's shoulder a squeeze before taking out her phone. "You two get that mower started. I'm going to have a good, long talk with your mom."

Sam could tell Edie wanted to argue, but Aunt Jo was like a bloodhound on the hunt, and it was no use trying to stop her.

The grass was even taller in the backyard than it was out front, like Edie had her own private jungle. They waded through without talking, making their way toward a dumpy shed, and the whole time Sam was thinking how he wished he had a better brain, because then he wouldn't be standing here saying nothing like a zombie.

It took both of them to pry open the rusty shed door. The mower was wedged into a mass of junk: a broken washing machine, a twisted car bumper, tires, tools, a pile of black garbage bags, a bike with missing handlebars, another bike with a piece of wood taped on in place of a seat.

170

"Sorry about this," Edie said. "I mean, this is probably the worst Saturday ever, right? Doing boring chores all day?"

She stared down at her shoes, which had little mouths where the soles had separated from the tops.

"It's not so bad," he said, surprised to find he was telling the truth. In fact, apart from going out fishing with Pa, he couldn't think of a single place he'd rather be than right here in this trash heap of a yard. "Do you ever ride those things?" He nodded toward the bikes, and only part of him was thinking how maybe he could use one later to slip away, because the other part of him was happy right where he was.

"Not for a really long time. I doubt they still work."

"Oh."

Once again, his brain died, and he was left standing there, sweating through the armpits of his shirt, despite the cold. Thankfully, Aunt Jo hollered, saying how that grass wasn't going to cut itself, and that sparked them both into action. They took turns, one of them using the mower out front, while the other hacked away at the grass in back with these huge clippers, which was kind of like trimming a giant's beard, if the giant's chin took up the whole backyard.

Every few minutes, Sam stole a look at his watch, counting down the time till he could see Pa. After they'd finished the grass and moved on to the gutters, Sam casually suggested that Aunt Jo drop him by school after lunch, since he needed to get something from his locker, and it might take him a while to find it, so she could just leave and come back in an hour. It sounded pretty reasonable in his head, but Aunt Jo didn't sound so sure. "You know the school's locked on Saturdays . . . but if you can't live without it, I can call Mr. Redding to let us in."

She started to dial Mr. Redding's number, and Sam panicked and said, "Never mind, I think maybe it's in my backpack after all."

Aunt Jo flashed him a suspicious look before returning her gaze to the overflowing gutters. Great. Sam's heart beat faster as he checked his watch yet again, and it slowly began to dawn on him that he might not make it to the tree in time to rescue Pa. But he had to make it, even if it meant stealing Baby Girl or riding a broken bike or running, in which case he should stop wasting time.

"Whoa, what's that?" He was momentarily distracted by Edie, who came out of the garage carrying a device that looked like a giant grabby hand, but with a motor and a dial on one end for controlling direction and speed.

"I call it the Gutter Destroyer 3000. It's a prototype. Also, I should probably change the name, because it's not actually supposed to destroy gutters, it's supposed to clean them."

Sam couldn't do anything but stare as Edie aimed the device at the overflowing gutters, the motor popping and whirring, and proceeded to grab and dump giant handfuls of wet leaves. Aunt Jo clapped, snapping pictures with her phone. After a while, Sam took a turn, but the giant robot arm proved harder to control than it looked. He nearly took out a window, and Aunt Jo had to duck once when he stepped in a hole, but eventually he got the hang of it.

By the time they'd cleaned out the gutters and bagged the leaves to Aunt Jo's satisfaction, it was 2:52 p.m. One hour before he had to be at the tree to rescue Pa. If he started running now, he might just make it.

"Jesus, Mary, and Joseph, look at the time." Aunt Jo clapped them both on the back, smiling way too wide for someone who'd just spent all day knee-deep in leaves. "Guess your science project will have to wait. How about three Saturday specials down at Gina's Diner? That's a chocolate milkshake, Gina's famous fried pickles, and all the chicken wings you can eat. Even you can't say no to wings." She dug her elbow into Sam's ribs, and his heart sank. 2:53 p.m.

"I thought I might try out one of those old bikes," Sam said, but Aunt Jo swatted down his words like flies.

"Nonsense. Nobody's starving to death on my watch. Now, you two go get washed up while I start the car. And remember, Baby Girl waits for no one."

Double great.

Sam followed Edie to the front door, but she stopped before letting him inside. "Sorry, it's kind of a mess. I haven't had time to clean up since . . . anyway, just try not to look at anything."

She opened the door, refusing to meet his eyes, and he stepped into a dimly lit living room. He had to admit, it was kind of a dump, with the saggy couch and stained carpet and the piles of dirty dishes. But it was also amazing. Not all the junk, but the other stuff, like the spinning model of the solar system dangling from the ceiling fan and the catapult on the kitchen table made from rubber bands, wooden spoons, and a whole lot of duct tape.

"It's for making breakfast," Edie said. She pressed a button and the catapult shot a beanbag that knocked over a cup that sent a marble spinning through a maze that triggered a lever that pulled a string that started the toaster.

"Holy crab cakes," he said, which was Pa's other favorite way of not cussing whenever Sam was around. "That is . . . freaking awesome!"

Edie shrugged and unplugged the toaster. "Not really. I just got bored. There's not much to do around here whenever Mom's gone." A sudden flash of anger crossed Edie's face, but it was gone as quickly as it had appeared.

"Oh."

Her cheeks got red, and she looked like she wanted to

bury her head in her hoodie and never come out again.

"Sorry."

"It's not your fault."

"Still."

A horn blasted out front, and Sam was annoyed but also kind of relieved.

"I guess we'd better go," he said, even though he didn't want to go, because of Pa, but he did want to get out of the house, because he had no idea what to say to make Edie feel better.

"Yeah, let me get the keys."

Sam said that Edie could have shotgun, partly because he needed time to plan, partly because he couldn't take any more awkward silences. 3:07 p.m. As they drove away, Sam felt like a prisoner on his way to death row, the way his skin started to itch and the way he knew that if he didn't find a way to escape soon, he was finished. But his heart grew lighter the more they drove, because he realized that Gina's Diner was a lot closer to school than he remembered, and maybe, if he could just slip away while the others were eating, he could still make it.

Despite the cool blast from the air conditioner as they walked inside, Sam could feel the sweat pooling in his armpits.

"Three Saturday specials," Aunt Jo called to a frazzled woman behind the counter, who echoed, "Three Saturday specials!" while at the same time pouring a coffee and giv-ing someone change from the register.

He waited till Edie and Aunt Jo had both settled into a booth before making his move. "I need to use the bath-room."

"Right back there," Aunt Jo said, pointing toward a doorway in the far corner next to an old jukebox. "Can't miss it. It's the one with the stuffed armadillo over the door."

"Thanks." Sam hesitated, feeling bad for leaving Edie all alone with Aunt Jo, but only for a second. "I might be a while. I'm not feeling too great."

"Need a Tums?" Aunt Jo said. "Think I've got an extra bottle in the car."

"That's okay. Just don't wait up." His cheeks burned as he hurried for the bathroom, mortified that Edie now thought he was having explosive diarrhea, but also relieved that he'd come up with a plan. And it was working.

He found the doorway with the stuffed armadillo but kept right on walking. This was it, and it was so easy. There was an exit just past the bathrooms. He slid outside, heart pounding, waiting for someone to catch him, but no one did. Some kid in an apron pushed past on his way inside, probably heading to work, and he didn't even bother to look up.

3:28 p.m.

The wind pulled at his clothes as he crossed the parking lot. He ducked between cars to make sure Aunt Jo wouldn't see him through the diner's side windows, and then, when he'd made it past the liquor store and the gas station, he ran. There were no sidewalks in Holler, Oklahoma, but the grass along the main road was smooth and flat. He picked up speed, absorbing the roar of the wind and the exhaust smoke and the spray of grit from passing semis. Pretty soon, it was like he was running the hundred-yard dash all over again, except this time he was in the lead and Andy Hamlin could eat his dust.

Despite the ache building in his calves and the wobble threatening his thighs, he pushed harder. So what if he couldn't catch his breath and his chest was burning and he'd probably pass out any second and never get up again?

3:35 p.m.

A sports car hit a pothole, spraying him with muddy sewer water, but he didn't care, because what was a little muddy water when he was about to rescue Pa?

3:37 p.m.

Some blue jays in the back of a truck laughed at him as they sped past, and one of them threw a beer bottle that shattered on the road and sent green shards of glass skittering past his ankles. So what? Jerks!

3:41 p.m.

He could see the school, and so he ran harder, even

177

though it was at the top of a grape-soda hill and he was about to suffocate and maybe have a heart attack, but this was happening. He was going to make it.

3:44 p.m.

He fell over a grape-soda curb and scraped his knee and he was bleeding and muddy, but so what? So what? All he had to do was get over this last hill and run past the playground and try not to die or pass out and . . .

3:46 p.m.

There it was. The tree, the dragonflies, the glint as they twitched their wings in unison like a school of passing fish. Without waiting for them to scatter, he removed the duct tape from his pack, leaving the rest behind, and dove into the hollow.

13

AS SOON AS THE DARKNESS got hold of him, he was falling. Zagging side to side, shoulders banging into rough bark, leaves and twigs and spidery legs snagging his hair, scraping at his face.

He dropped to the hard ground and knew right away that something had gone wrong. His fingers touched cracked dirt and brittle grass. The sun beat down, burning his eyes, and the air was dry and violent and full of dust. He sat up, head throbbing, and looked out at a sea of swaying grass burnt brown by the sun. Beyond that, a ruin, like something out of Ancient Greece, only way less fancy.

"Take me back," Sam said, because he could feel the presence of One-Eye or the Boy or whoever he was nearby. "I'm not supposed to be here. Take me to Pa." He shoved the roll of duct tape farther up his arm as a faraway voice called in answer.

"Hey, slowpoke! You eat turtle soup for breakfast? Because I've never seen anyone run so slow!"

A teenager with cropped hair and overalls burst from between two broken columns and leaped to the grass. It was a young Aunt Jo, followed by a slightly older Pa, racing after her through the knee-high grass, wielding a stick like a sword.

Pa was fast, but Aunt Jo was faster. Sam couldn't believe the way she ran, like she had lightning bolts trapped in her sneakers. He watched her leap over a weed the size of a warthog without so much as breaking her stride, and then he rubbed the dizziness from his head and took off after them.

By the time he caught up, Pa and Aunt Jo were sitting beside a rusty oil rig, sharing a can of Orange Crush.

"Pa!" he said, but Pa didn't hear him. "We have to go!" He shouted and tried to grab Pa's arm, but it was another one of the Boy's tricks. Like last time with Mama, his hand slid right through.

Pa grinned over at Aunt Jo, taking a swig of soda. He was maybe eighteen or nineteen by the looks of it. "So you really did it? You signed up for the army?" Pa passed the can to Aunt Jo, then leaned back against a concrete support.

She took a sip, eyes focused on the clouds looming low on the horizon. "I had to. I can't stay here. Besides, they said they'd fast-track me for pilot's training."

"What did Pops say?"

Aunt Jo's expression darkened. "What do you think?"

Pa plucked a piece of dead grass and slid it between his

teeth. "I think Pops is as stubborn as a donkey and half as smart."

"What about you? You moving out for good this time? Pops said you got a place down on the swamps in Louisiana. He didn't seem too happy about it."

"Don't see much reason to stay. Not once you're gone."

Aunt Jo leaned back and studied the clouds. "It'll be different, not having you around."

"We'll still talk. I'm not moving to Timbuktu."

"I might be. And after that . . . well, Pops said I'm not welcome here again, not if I join up."

A gust of wind rolled over the dead grass, making it rise and fall in waves.

"But we'll still be us, no matter what and no matter where." Pa bumped her shoulder and she bumped him back. "Right? You and me against the world."

"Yeah, we'll still be us." Aunt Jo kept her gaze on the sky, following the slow circle of a passing hawk. "I think Pops hates me."

"He doesn't hate you," Pa said. "He sure hates me, though, if that makes you feel any better."

"I can't be the person he wants me to be," Aunt Jo said.

Pa looked at her, and it was so strange to see them sitting there, just a few years older than Sam. So real and sad and yet still hopeful about the world.

"But you're you. And, sure, you're annoying as heck, and you fish like a girl, but—"

"Shut up." She was laughing.

"Come on, race you back?"

"If you think you can take the humiliation."

"Oh, I can take it."

With that, Pa stole the head start, Aunt Jo on his heels, and the world collapsed in around Sam. It was like everything, the field, the ruin, even the sky and the clouds were sucked into a black hole, and Sam was hurtling along its center. He tried to shout for the Boy, to demand that he be taken to Pa, his pa, but he couldn't do anything but scream.

He landed facedown in the mud.

"Take me to Pa!" he shouted, scrambling to his feet and swiping the muck from his face and mouth.

"You do realize that you're in no position to make demands." The Boy was leaning against a tree nearby, twirling a set of whiskers that had sprouted from his cheeks. Though he still wore Pa's face, it had taken on a distinctly feline quality, his lips curving up in the center and his pupils narrowing into slits.

"Who are you? Why are you doing this?"

The Boy watched Sam, eyes glinting in the light filtering in through the treetops. "People die, and then they move on. Except sometimes they don't, or can't. That's why I'm here."

"Are you Death?"

"What a nasty word. Like I said, think of me as your guide. I show the living what they need to see in order to let go. And you will let go. Trust me. I always get the job done in the end."

"And what if I don't?"

The Boy's body flickered. For a moment he was a skeleton draped with bits of seaweed and rotting skin, then the Boy, then something in between.

"You will. Eventually."

"Take me to Pa. Now." But before Sam could finish, the Boy was gone. A twig snapped behind him, and Sam turned to find Pa, his pa. A second later, he was wrapped up in Pa's arms, and all the confusion and questions and doubt of the past few days faded away.

"It's been so long. I didn't think I'd ever see you again." Pa wiped his face, and Sam saw that he'd been crying.

"But it's only been a day."

Pa looked ready to argue, but Sam wasn't wasting any time.

"Here, quick. Wrap this around your arm." Sam used the duct tape to bind his left arm to Pa's right, and Pa made sure it was extra tight, wrapping that tape as fast as he could, not bothering to ask questions. Sam could tell he understood.

"Ready?" Pa said, staring at the hollow, which stood just a few feet away, gaping at them like an evil mouth.

"Ready."

"You first."

It should have been impossible for them both to climb into a hole that was no bigger than a dinner plate, but the wood seemed to grow and stretch around them. His plan was working. As soon as Sam's head and shoulders had been swallowed by the wet darkness, he was flying straight up, a fierce wind at his back. Only this time, Sam wasn't the least bit scared, because he could feel Pa at his side. They flew faster and faster, Sam's stomach lurching up his throat, and then the sunlight assaulted his eyes and he dropped to the hard, dead earth.

His fingers spread out, feeling the solid ground beneath him. "Pa!" he called, head spinning, certain he had somehow been lost or left behind. Then he heard a groan followed by a tugging on his arm, and there was Pa pulling him tight against his chest.

When they were done hugging, which wasn't for a while, Sam turned and saw that the hollow had closed up. Just like that. It had all been . . . so easy. Almost like the Boy had let them escape.

He looked at Pa, and he never wanted to stop looking, because here he was, back in the real world, and Sam could feel him and smell him and he wasn't a dream or even a ghost. Pa reached in his pocket and took out his knife, the one with a green enamel gator on the handle. He whittled away at their duct tape handcuffs till they split apart, then Sam set to tearing off the rest.

"Best to do it in one go, like a Band-Aid," Pa said, and Sam ripped at the tape, only wincing a little when it peeled off the tiny hairs on his arm.

Pa stood up, wobbly-legged, and took in the field and the school and the gravel road sending up clouds of white dust. "Never thought I'd come back here," Pa said, rubbing the side of his neck. "I never asked, but how's your aunt Jo?" He looked down at his hands, picking some of the grit from beneath his nails. "Guess I've got some things to tell you about your aunt, why she stayed away. Don't know how much she's said, but I owe her an apology. I was no better than Pops, when it comes right down to it. I never should've treated her like that, even if she did . . . well, maybe we'd better head on into town. A conversation like this requires adequate refreshment."

"I already know, Pa. She told me." Sam thought back to the memory the Boy had shown him of Pa and Aunt Jo, a brother and sister against the world. He'd been wrong before. Pa wasn't just some stranger to her. They really were family. "And she forgives you."

Pa thought on that a while, chewing his lip the way he did whenever he was trying not to cry at sad movies. "All right then. What now?" Pa looked up at the sky and out at the great expanse of grass, like he was seeing it all for the first time.

What now? Sam had a million questions, like why hadn't Pa ever told him about Mama or the Colonel, and how did it feel to be dead, and why hadn't Pa trusted Sam enough to tell him the truth? About his stories, Aunt Jo, everything. Instead, he squeezed Pa's hand again, double-checking he was real, and said, "Guess we head back to the diner. Aunt Jo's probably wondering where I am."

"And me? She'll likely have more than a few questions if I wander in off the street, good as new." Sam hadn't considered that. He hadn't thought about anything beyond getting Pa out of the tree and back where he belonged. His palms prickled at the strange reality of what had happened, and he fought against the sick feeling that at any moment he could lose it all.

"Maybe you should wait outside, till I get a chance to explain."

"And how do you plan on doing that? Not that I'm questioning your abilities, but that'll be one mighty strange conversation, don't you think?"

"True. Maybe it's best if she sees you for herself."

Pa let out a long breath, but nodded. "Better to rip off the Band-Aid, huh? All right, let's get this over with."

With Pa's arm around his shoulders, they headed back

186

toward the diner. Even though Pa was here and everything had worked out, Sam's heart hadn't stopped pounding. They made it over the first hill, and then Pa stopped, overlooking the dinky playground with its rusty rocking horses and beat-up jungle gym.

"Pa, you okay?"

"Yeah, just let me catch my breath."

Except Sam could tell that Pa wasn't okay. He doubled over, clutching his chest and wheezing, but the air wouldn't go in. Then Sam saw the curve in Pa's neck, like someone had twisted it around too far and then tried to smooth it out again. It hadn't been like that before, he would swear to it. It hadn't been that way since the day of the accident.

Pa sank to his knees, eyes shiny with fear, and Sam couldn't do anything but watch as cuts and bruises appeared on Pa's skin.

"No, Pa! What's happening?"

He held onto Pa's shoulders as Pa slid to the ground, shaking and scared, and Sam didn't know one single thing to do about it.

The cat slithered past Sam's arm and changed in one smooth motion into the Boy. "He can't come back. Not the way he used to be." His feline features were gone, and he looked exactly like twelve-year-old Pa, except with no trace of his signature grin. "Unfortunate, I know, but that's life for you. Well, to be more accurate, that's death. I thought it would be more convincing if you saw it for yourself."

"He's hurting! Make it stop."

"The doorway's open. One-way access only. You can send him back any time you like." The sunlight shifted, making the Boy look older than he had before, the shadows cutting deep lines down his face.

Pa moaned, and Sam didn't stop to question or mourn his loss. Pa was in pain, and he had to make it stop. "Come on, take my arm."

Using strength he didn't know he had, Sam lifted Pa to his feet and half dragged him back to the tree. He could tell the doorway was open again because he could smell home on the other side.

"Just him," said the Boy. "Until tomorrow."

Sam didn't argue.

"No," Pa pleaded, but then the pain grew so intense his plea gave way to a scream.

"Please, Pa. Just go!"

Pa cupped Sam's face, pressing their foreheads together for one impossible moment, then he turned and climbed shakily back into the tree. Sam felt it the instant the hollow closed, because the air turned dry and empty, and the connection he had felt between him and Pa, the feverish prickling in his palms, had broken.

"You're evil," Sam said, turning around, half expecting the Boy to have disappeared, but there he was.

"If you say so." He shrugged, standing alone on the grass, looking small and cruel and like nothing at all. A sudden surge of anger rushed up Sam's throat, and he lunged, shoving the Boy hard to the ground. And then he was punching him. Each punch hurt his hands, but he didn't care if he broke every finger, and then he saw the Boy's face staring up at him and stumbled back, collapsing on the ground and choking on his own ugly tears. It was Pa's face, but it wasn't, but it still was.

They sat there for a while, both sprawled out on the grass looking bloody and crumpled, and the Boy didn't say anything, which was good, because then Sam probably would have kept right on punching him.

"How long?" he said, when everything warring inside him had settled down enough to talk. "How long before the doorway closes for good?"

The Boy watched Sam, considering his answer. "Soon."

A cool gust pushed against Sam's body, bringing a few rain droplets as a warning. Sam ignored it. "What if I wanted to stay there?"

"Stay where?" the Boy said. Sam didn't bother to answer; he could tell the Boy understood. "There is no *there*. Not in the way you mean. It's a fantasy. Think of it like a waiting room between this world and the next."

"But I've been there. I've seen it."

"You've seen what I wanted you to see. Besides, it's not

a place for the living. Once the doorway between worlds closes for good, there's no going back."

"Then why? What's the point of it all? What's the point of you?"

The Boy smiled, but this time it wasn't cruel so much as bittersweet. "I told you: you've been given a rare opportunity. The chance to say goodbye."

"What if I don't? What if I never say goodbye?"

A siren whirred to life in the distance, along with the low roll of thunder.

"That's your choice," the Boy said, and then the sky opened up, burying them under a barrage of stinging raindrops.

THE RAIN HAD LET UP and the sky had turned a rusty orange by the time Sam made it back to Gina's Diner. So much for it never raining in Holler, although maybe that was because the rain clouds had followed him here all the way from Louisiana. From down the street, he could see the lights of a police cruiser washing the wet cars and pavement in shades of blue and red. He didn't want to go back and face Aunt Jo, but the sooner he got it over with, the better.

Aunt Jo was talking to this police officer who smelled like greasy hamburgers and way too much cologne, and Sam stood there like a blue jay waiting for her to notice him. The officer was saying how in most cases the kid had just wandered off, and how they'd drive around and see what they could see, but how she shouldn't worry. Her eyes drifted to the left and locked on Sam. Her face registered confusion and then relief, but she didn't pull him into a hug the way Pa might have. She didn't yell at him either.

"This him?" the officer said, following Aunt Jo's gaze. She nodded, and then the officer said some stuff into a walkie, and Aunt Jo thanked him for his time, and he drove away.

Sam watched him go, dreading what came next.

Aunt Jo drew in a long breath and let it out again. "You want to tell me where you were?"

"Not really." He regretted it the second he said it, because he was being a huge blue jay and because Pa would be disappointed and because, if he was being totally honest, Aunt Jo wasn't all that bad. But he was also tired, and he couldn't right now; he just couldn't.

Aunt Jo looked him over, and he could see a conversation playing out in her head, but all she said was, "Okay. I get it."

"You do?"

He expected her to say something pointless and inspirational, like from her positive affirmations tape, but instead she said, "It's a lot. With your pa gone. It's a lot for me, and I know it's a lot for you. You need your space, and I get that. I'll try to be better about it."

Sam didn't know what to say, so he said nothing. Then he noticed Edie leaning against the ice machine like she wasn't sure where she was supposed to be.

"Just promise me one thing." The sun peeked through a gap in the clouds, and Aunt Jo shielded her eyes. "If you need to go somewhere, or you just need to take a walk, tell me first. I'm not a prison guard, and you're old enough to

192

watch out for yourself. But I'm responsible for you now, so I need to know where to find you. Deal?"

She reached out her hand. They shook on it, which was more painful than it sounds, since Aunt Jo had a grip like a boa constrictor. Still, he was glad when it was done. After that, they sat back down and ate, and nobody asked him where he'd gone or why, and he was glad, and then they all went home.

Edie stayed at their house again, since her mom wasn't answering her phone, and they talked about their project some and then made tacos with Tabasco and extra jalapeños. Sam and Edie did the dishes, and then they ate ice cream sundaes for dessert and played go fish, which was kind of funny, because Aunt Jo had the fishing channel on in the background.

When it was time for bed, Edie went to her room. Sam and Aunt Jo headed up the stairs, and then Aunt Jo stopped and said, "I miss him, too, you know."

And Sam didn't say anything, but he looked right into Aunt Jo's eyes and nodded, because the truth was that he did know. Pa was her brother and her friend and they'd known each other their whole lives. She had as much right to miss Pa as he did.

"Good night," Aunt Jo said after a while. She headed up the stairs, and Sam watched her go. He still felt like an alien on a strange planet, in a house that would never quite be home. He stood there in the cool shadows, breathing in the now familiar scents. Earlier today, he'd thought that Pa would be here with him. And now?

He'd tried to rescue Pa and failed. He'd spent all day thinking of ways to make it work, ways to prove the Boy wrong, but once again his brain had let him down.

He closed his eyes and pretended he was in the little white house on stilts, the swamp burbling away outside. He imagined the sounds and smells, wet wood, clinking wind chimes. It all seemed so distant, like a watercolor painting slowly fading away in the sun.

The next morning, Aunt Jo woke them up bright and early to work in the garden. She fed them pancakes and bacon first, with soda instead of juice, and then sent Sam and Edie out back to pull weeds.

Pa had never once woken up on a Sunday before ten, unless he was going fishing, but that was different. By the time noon rolled around, they'd weeded and planted and watered. Sam enjoyed the work, partly because Edie was there helping him, partly because it gave him a chance to think. The weight of losing Pa—again—had rested heavy on his shoulders all night, like a hot, sweaty blanket. He couldn't see any way that Pa could stay, not if it meant that he'd be in constant pain.

"Earth to Sam," Edie said, coming up to stand beside

him. "You've been staring at that rock for five minutes."

"It's a pretty cool rock," Sam said, looking over at Edie, who had a strand of purple hair clinging to her cheek. Actually, he hadn't realized he'd been staring.

"True. As far as rocks go, it's basically the coolest."

"Exactly."

Edie laughed, which made Sam laugh too. It felt good to get out of his head for a minute, even if he knew he should be focused on Pa.

Sam picked dried mud from the spade he'd been holding, and turned to Edie. "Can I ask you something?"

"Sure, anything."

He drew in a deep breath. "When your dad left, did you ever think about going with him?" The question had been bugging him for a while now. As far as he could tell, Edie's mom was never home, plus she was an addict. Wouldn't it be better for her to stay with her dad?

Edie's mouth opened, but she didn't answer. The blood drained from her cheeks, and he suddenly wished he could erase the past few seconds and go back to talking about rocks.

"Sorry. It's none of my business."

"No, it's okay," she said, her voice quiet. "He didn't really give me a choice. He just left one day, and Mom only found out because our neighbor saw him packing up his car."

"Oh."

"We didn't even know where he was at first, but then Mom hired some lady to track him down and she found him at this motel in California." She started gathering up the garden supplies, not looking at Sam while she finished her story. "I thought about going out there, some time when my mom wasn't around. I even saved enough money for a bus ticket." She let out a long breath, and her face was so sad and beautiful, Sam wanted to take her hand, but didn't. "I never used it. What's the point? I already know he doesn't want to see me."

With that, a breeze blew in, rustling the leaves on the tiny trees in Aunt Jo's backyard. Sam could feel that the moment had passed, but somehow Edie's story had given him the answer he needed.

"Hey, wanna go inside for a while? I'm starving." Edie smiled, but he could see the sadness lingering at the edges of her mouth.

"Sure thing. Here, I'll put that stuff away."

Edie went inside, and he put the tools she'd gathered up back in the shed. He was glad for the moment to himself, because he needed time to think. Edie couldn't visit her dad, because he didn't want to see her. With Pa it was different. Pa needed him. True, he couldn't see a way to bring Pa back to this world, but what if there was a way that he could stay in the other world? The Boy had said it was impossible, that the other place wasn't fit for the living, but what if? What if he'd been wrong? What if he'd just been saying that to trick Sam into letting go?

Even if it wasn't possible, he had to try. That would be his new plan. His heart beat faster at the possibility and the weight from the night before lifted off his chest. It wasn't over. Pa wasn't lost.

He'd started to head back inside when he tripped over something in the shed that turned out to be an old bike. He touched the handlebars and squeezed the tires, surprised to find them full of air.

"Haven't ridden that thing in years," Aunt Jo said, coming up behind him. She looked him over, like she had in the diner parking lot, and said, "Feel like giving her a spin?"

Sam couldn't believe his luck, but the hollow wouldn't open for another three hours. "Maybe later. I think Edie's ready for lunch."

"Suit yourself."

They ate leftover tacos with extra Tabasco, and then Aunt Jo put them to work again washing all the windows. By the time they were done, Sam could barely lift his arms, and he slumped down on the couch next to Edie.

"I could sleep for a week," she said, and Sam's hand accidentally touched her arm, but he pulled it away fast, so maybe she didn't notice.

"Me too."

The ceiling fan clicked overhead—*click, click, click*—but

Sam was too tired to turn it off. He let his muscles relax for a few seconds, knowing he'd have to hop on the bike soon and get back to Pa. Pa. Who knew how much longer the hollow would stay open. Would this be the day that he would stay with Pa for good? Weirdly, the thought hadn't occurred to him until this moment. Staying with Pa would mean leaving Edie and Aunt Jo and everything else behind. It was what he wanted, to be back with Pa, but it was all happening so fast.

"You want to work on our science fair project? We could finish up our design." Edie reached for the notes they'd been working on earlier.

Sam checked his watch. "Maybe another time."

"Oh, okay." She put the notebook back on the coffee table. "We could watch TV. Do you guys get anything besides the fishing channel?"

"Actually, I kind of have to go."

"Now?" She pushed up onto her elbows, and so did Sam.

"Yeah, it's just . . . I have this thing."

"Oh. Where are you going?"

"Nowhere. I mean, Aunt Jo said I could try out her old bike."

"I could go with you."

Sam stared at his knees. The longer he didn't say anything, the more the air tightened around his throat.

Edie's cheeks turned red, and she started talking fast,

gathering up her things. "No, it's fine. I should go home anyway. I totally understand if you want to be alone. I have homework to do and laundry and stuff, so it's probably for the best."

"It's not you. It's just . . ."

"You have a thing. Got it. No worries. I'll see you tomorrow, right? After school?"

"Sure. I mean, definitely."

"Okay, so . . . bye, then." And just like that, she hurried out the door and was gone. Aunt Jo walked out after her and, when she came back in, Sam asked if he could borrow her bike. She said yes, and she asked why he didn't invite Edie, but he couldn't come up with a good answer, and Aunt Jo didn't push it, and then he left.

Getting to the tree was a lot easier on his bike, except he kept getting sprayed by trucks barreling down the main road, and he was pretty sure someone would run him over, but they didn't, but he did get honked at twice. The closer he got to the tree, the more the weight of his plan ballooned to monster size in his mind. This was really happening. He was going to stay with Pa.

There had to be a way.

First, he thought about tying himself to something, like one of the old posts on the dock, but then he remembered what the Boy had said. If the swamp wasn't real, if it could change shapes whenever the Boy wanted, then tying himself

199

to something in that world wouldn't work. Then what? He could tie himself to Pa, but that would end in Pa getting sucked back to this world again, and he couldn't risk that.

Think. There had to be a way. When he reached the school parking lot, he hopped a curb and pedaled hard up the hill.

The tree came into view, dead leaves rattling in the wind, and suddenly he knew the answer.

The tree was in this world and the other one. It was the anchor, the doorway between the worlds. If he could tether himself to the tree, when he was on the other side, then the invisible force or the Boy or whatever it was wouldn't be able to drag him back.

Maybe.

Okay, it was a long shot, but it was also his only hope. His palms prickled with possibility.

He reached the hollow at 3:45 p.m. on the dot. It wasn't until he got closer that he noticed something different about the tree. No dragonflies. Just a few dead bug bodies littered here and there on the grass.

His heart strained in his chest as he climbed off his bike and pressed a hand to the bark. It was dry, brittle. He squeezed his head into the hollow, fear now pulsing in his brain. Was this it? Had the hollow closed up without warning?

He pushed in deeper, waiting for the horrible moment

when his forehead would touch rough wood, but it never came. The hollow was still open. He forced his shoulders inside, wiggling to the point where he usually tipped forward and started falling. Today, he didn't feel that strange force drawing him in. Instead, he had to climb.

Down and down, using twigs and vines as handholds. As he went, the tunnel grew narrower, almost like he could feel it closing in around him. Like whatever magic had been holding the tunnel open was slowly draining away.

By the time he felt the muggy air on his cheeks and saw a sliver of sunlight up ahead, the tunnel had grown so narrow he had to dig his fingernails into the soft wood to keep moving. Finally, he dropped out on the other side, plucking the splinters from his palms. He took a moment to catch his breath, searching the stooping tupelos for any signs of the Boy.

A warm breeze whispered through the dense tree cover, bringing with it the familiar scent of swamp water and the soft tinkling of Pa's beer-can chimes. Still scanning for any signs of One-Eye or the Boy, Sam made his way through the muddy underbrush toward the water. Pa was there, boots dangling off the edge of the dock. As soon as he saw Sam, he shot to his feet and waved. Before Sam could move, Pa hopped in the canoe and was gliding steadily toward him. Despite the canoe moving of its own accord, Pa couldn't wait, so he used his hands like paddles. A moment later, he was lifting Sam up and holding him tight and saying how he'd never let him go, not this time, not ever.

Sam brought out his trusty roll of duct tape, which was half as big as last time, and he told Pa his plan to tape himself to the tree and wait for the hollow to close. They worked fast, making big loops around Sam's belly and fastening him nice and snug to the ancient trunk. Pa paused after a while to examine their work so far, and that was when his forehead crinkled.

"You say the hollow only opens once a day?" he said, eyes deep in thought.

"That's right. At 3:45 p.m. The time . . ."

"Oh . . . right. The time of my accident." Pa nodded, but Sam could tell something else was troubling him. "What about tomorrow? And the day after that? Will we have to wrap you up like this every day? And what will you do about school, and Aunt Jo?"

Sam shook his head. "Pa, none of that matters now. Besides, the hollow won't keep opening up forever. The Boy told me. Pretty soon, I won't have to worry about getting zapped back. It'll just be you and me, here on the swamp." This seemed to worry Pa more than anything. His gaze drifted up through the treetops, and they both saw the sun hanging low on the horizon, painting the leaves in vibrant reds and oranges.

"Pa! Keep going! It's already sunset." Pa snapped out of

it, and together they wrapped Sam up tighter than a burrito in a chokehold.

They'd just finished off the last of the tape when Sam heard a rush of water followed by plodding footsteps, and there, emerging from the giant leaves, was the Colonel. He stood silent, all fifteen angry feet of him, not two yards away, an arrow protruding from his skull. The Colonel watched Sam with his glowing yellow eyes, then hung his head, and to Sam's extreme surprise, Pa bent down and gave his snout a pat.

"What happened to him?" Sam said, because Pa had never explained how the Colonel had ended up here or how come he hadn't seemed all that surprised to see the arrow.

Pa plunked down on a nest of vines next to Sam, his eyes taking on the faraway, dreamlike quality they always got when he was getting ready to tell a story. A mammoth dragonfly perched on a nearby toadstool, tilting its massive wings to soak up the last rays of sun. Other insects joined in, mosquitoes trailing two-inch stingers and cicadas creeping down from the treetops, silencing their rattle just long enough to listen.

"It happened a few weeks back, maybe longer now. You were at school and I was out fishing like always." Pa settled in, like this was any other day, not a matter of life and death. "Trailed the Colonel down to Mermaid Cove and beyond.

I'd tracked him a fair bit in the past, but never this long or this far. He moved in these lazy zigzags, keeping close to the surface, and after a while I decided he was doing it for my benefit. Almost like he wanted me to follow. I told him stories as we went, of all the times I'd tried to find him, and other stories too, and the strange thing was, he seemed to listen." The Colonel snorted, and Pa gave his snout another scratch. "We were floating and chatting, and the sun was warm, but not too warm, and the shade fell in all the right spots, and it was one of those lazy afternoons you hope might stretch on forever, but it never does. In retrospect, I should have made sure we were alone."

The Colonel tensed, showing off his teeth, and the insects in the audience shifted in their seats. "I'd brought a few sandwiches, turkey and Tabasco, nothing special, and I pulled up on that sandy beach over by the red cliffs. You know the one. I thought the Colonel would have gone his merry way by then, and so I was chomping on my sandwiches, enjoying the pretty weather, when I heard the water slosh and there he was. This monstrous shape emerging from the depths—no offense," he added, nodding down at the Colonel. "Looking like he'd stepped straight out of prehistoric times. And he moseyed on over, like it was no big deal, his face all rutted and weathered and fierce."

Sam held his breath, too wrapped up in the story to notice the shadows spilling over the swamp and swallowing up the last hints of sun. "I thought for sure I was a goner. I waited for his massive jaws to chew me to bits, but they didn't. After a while, I decided he must want to be friends, and so I tossed him one of my turkey-and-Tabasco sandwiches. He snapped it up, licking his lips, and then I fed him a second and a third, before breaking out laughing. It was too darn wild. All this time chasing him, all those stories, and it turned out he wouldn't hurt a fly. That was when it happened.

"What I hadn't noticed, amid all the fear and wonder, was the lone hunter sneaking up behind us through the trees. I didn't hear the arrow coming till it was already too late, and by then all I could do was get out of the way as the Colonel thrashed." A moan escaped from the Colonel's throat, and Sam could taste the ache of it deep down in his gut. "The worst part was, that hunter hadn't even been looking for the Colonel. Didn't know the first thing about the legend. He was some nobody out-of-towner planning to sell any gator he could find for spare parts, and he laughed, actually laughed when I told him what he'd done."

The insects moved in closer, gathering around the Colonel's feet, waiting to hear the conclusion of Pa's story. "By the time he was finished laughing, the Colonel was dead, and I knew one thing for certain. I might not have been able to save him. Heck, maybe I was the reason he was dead, but I'd be damned if that blue jay would be the one to put an end to a legend. I warned him to get away, but his expression turned hard. He thrust his crossbow in my face, threatening to put an arrow between my eyes just like he'd done with the Colonel. I had no choice but to spring into action."

Sam leaned closer, hanging on Pa's every word.

"He was stronger, that much was clear, but I was quicker on my feet. I grabbed the only weapon I had, my trusty bottle of Tabasco, and shook a hefty helping in his face. While he was busy sputtering and stumbling, I dragged the Colonel back into the swamp and watched his body disappear into the deep, muddy water. I couldn't save his life, but at least I made sure his killer didn't take home any trophies.

"After that, I headed straight for Bobby Joe's, telling them all about the out-of-towner who was running around the swamps shooting off arrows. Couldn't hit a tree stump at point-blank range, I told 'em. So when that blue jay came in a few hours later, spouting off about killing the Colonel and me stealing the body, not a single soul believed him. Bobby Joe and the others laughed him right out of town, and so the legend went on. I even talked about spotting the Colonel a few times after that, and the funny thing was, other people saw him too. Like he really was still alive, which I guess ain't too far from the truth, since his legend lives on."

As Pa's final words faded, two bright lights flared to life, coming from the far side of the swamp. Sam heard the low rumble of a car engine, which meant they must be headlights. The engine's distinct growl and pop reminded Sam of Pa's '68 Sunbird. He glanced over at Pa, but it was like looking at a stranger. The harsh lights brought out the fear on Pa's face, fear he'd never seen there before, and the Colonel suddenly whipped around, snapping and snarling.

At the same time, Sam felt the pull behind his belly button. Pa grabbed him with both hands, holding him fast. "Don't worry. I won't let you go." The tugging grew stronger, drawing him toward the hollow, but the tape would hold, he knew it would. It had held to Pa yesterday, hadn't it? The lights flared, making Sam's eyes water. His hands began to slip from Pa's grasp, the tape stretching as he was sucked toward the gaping hole that seemed to be opening wider by the second.

"It's too strong!" he said, but then his words were ripped from his throat, and despite Pa's grip and the tape binding him tight to the tree, an invisible tongue coiled around his middle and jerked him into the darkness.

The last thing he heard before hitting the ground on the other side was Pa's voice calling his name.

15

THAT NIGHT, DEFEATED AND EXHAUSTED and at a loss for what to do next, Sam found Aunt Jo looking at pictures in the living room with all the lights turned off except for one ugly yellow lamp. He peered over her shoulder at the faded photos with the old-timey white borders.

"Did he really kick you out, when you went to join the army?"

She was holding a picture of Pops lounging on the front porch of the yellow house, a beer in one hand and a newspaper in the other. "He wasn't a mean man, not really, except when he was drinking. But he knew how he wanted people to be." Aunt Jo sighed, her gaze lost in the photo. "And I never measured up. Couldn't be his perfect, pretty daughter. And your pa didn't measure up either, but in his own way. Misfits, the both of us. In the end, we left home and never came back."

"But you're here now," Sam pointed out.

"True. Pops passed not long after I lost my leg, and I came back here to settle things. Ended up staying." She laid down the photo and began to sort the piles she'd made

208

into neat stacks. "Must be hard for you here. I know it's not much like your old home, but I hope one day that'll change."

Sam didn't answer. The truth was, this place *could* feel like home someday, and that's what scared him. If he let go of Pa, then it would be like turning his back on his memory. It would be the same as saying that Pa wasn't as important as his new life with Edie and Aunt Jo. But his plan had failed, if you could even call it a plan. What had made him think that taping himself to the tree would work? And where did that leave him now? He couldn't bring Pa back, and he didn't see how he could stay.

He needed more time. There had to be a way he could stay with Pa, and he was going to find it.

Later, tossing and turning in his bed, he dreamed of the Boy and One-Eye, and something in between, a hybrid grinning cat-boy with a single glowing eye and razor-thin teeth. He dreamed of headlights cutting through the darkness, seizing Pa and the Colonel in their cold, inescapable glare. He dreamed of Mama and Pops and a young Aunt Jo racing Pa across fields of dead grass. And he dreamed of Pa calling his name, and of the Boy, hidden away in the cool emptiness of the tree, reminding him that once the hollow was closed, he could never go back.

He woke up sweaty and sore, and no closer to finding a way to stay with Pa.

When he finally managed to get dressed and slump down at the kitchen table the next morning, he felt like a bus had run over his face, then backed up and run over him again. He ate cold pancakes for breakfast, which weren't as good as cold pizza, but not as gross as he'd expected.

He didn't know what to pack to get ready for his visit to Pa that afternoon, so he stuffed his backpack full of general emergency essentials: duct tape, obviously, plus a multitool, a length of paracord, waterproof matches, and a freeze-dried ice cream sandwich because just in case.

He was heading for the front door, head aching, when Aunt Jo called him back.

"Hang on. I almost forgot." Aunt Jo dug around in her purse for a while and then produced a check written out in big swirly strokes similar to Pa's. "For the community science fair. Just give it to Mr. Redding; he'll know where to send it. You two are staying late again today, right?"

Sam swallowed and took the check. "Right, thanks."

"Good for you. Sorry you're stuck on the bus this morning, but I'm picking up that early shift at the Shop 'n' Save, and we sure could use the money. Have a good day."

"You too."

Just then, the bus's air brakes whooshed outside, and Sam ran for it. When they got to Edie's stop, she wasn't there. He wondered if it had anything to do with him blowing her off the day before. No way. It wasn't like she liked him, not like-liked him. Even if she did, he wasn't some sexy movie star that girls would skip school over. He was just regular old Sam.

As proof, he saw Edie running down the street just as the bus pulled away, and he shouted for the driver to stop. And he did stop, after another half a block, which gave everyone on the bus time to stare and snicker as Edie ran to catch up. When she finally made it on, she sank into the seat next to Sam, and this tiny thrill ran through his body, but he ignored it, because how grape soda was that?

Edie's hair looked like a nest of wild thistles, probably thanks to the wind, and she was wearing the same clothes as the day they'd met, but with new stripy socks that matched her hair.

"Rough night?" Sam said. Partly because she looked like she hadn't slept and partly to cover up all the whispering from the back of the bus. Thankfully, the air brakes did their whoosh thing and the bus started off down the bumpy road, which drowned out most of the laughter.

Edie nodded. She looked like maybe she was too tired to answer.

"So I guess your mom's home again."

"Yup."

"Where was she?"

Edie shrugged.

"Did she bring you anything cool, at least?"

She snapped the elastic on her new stripy socks.

"Nice."

They sat in silence for a while, listening to the drone of the motor and the crunch of the tires as the bus moved from a paved road to a gravel one.

"I'm just gonna close my eyes for a bit. I'm still listening, though, in case you want to talk," Edie said.

"Okay."

She didn't close her eyes. "We're actually working on our project after school this time, aren't we?"

"Yeah."

"You promised."

Sam felt the heat creeping into his cheeks, but he forced himself not to look away. "I know. I'll be there."

"All right. Just don't run off this time."

She turned away from him, and then she did close her eyes, and he spent the rest of the ride finishing the homework he hadn't bothered to do the night before. His answers were mostly chicken scratch because of all the bumping, but at least he wouldn't get zeroes.

Edie was still asleep when the bus pulled up to Holler Junior High. Sam nudged her shoulder, and she woke with a start, glasses askew.

"Sorry. We're here."

She gathered up her stuff, but they had to wait until everybody else got off since the line had already started moving and nobody was in the mood to let them in.

Class that day was pretty boring. They were done with the owl barf and were talking instead about the Civil War. Usually Sam liked history, since it was basically a bunch of stories, and sometimes they were super gross and bloody. But Mr. Redding had one of those deep voices that makes you want to fall asleep or hit your head on the desk or, at the very least, think about something else, and so Sam spent most of the morning staring out the window thinking about Pa. Who knew how much longer the doorway would stay open? He had to figure something out today.

Edie was quiet during lunch: gritty hamburgers, tater tots, and a hunk of iceberg lettuce. She said she wasn't hungry like the day before, but she ate his lettuce and a few of his tater tots, and she made a pickle sandwich from his bottom bun.

"We don't have to work on the project today. I mean, if you don't want to."

Those words perked her right up. "You're not trying to skip out on me again are you?" Her eyes blazed behind her glasses and, even though she was cute, she also looked kind of scary. Of course, he was trying to skip out on her, but not because he didn't like her, which he didn't, but still.

"No. Just if you're tired or something," Sam said.

"I'm fine."

"You look tired."

"Thanks a lot."

"I didn't mean it like . . . oh."

Edie gave him a half smile that said she was joking.

When class started again, Sam went right back to staring out the window until Mr. Redding said three words that got his attention: *Abraham Lincoln* and *ghost*.

"After dying of what we now believe to be typhoid fever at age eleven, Willie Lincoln was embalmed and laid out in the Green Room," Mr. Redding said, stroking his ugly white mustache. "His mother, Mary Lincoln, was so stricken with grief that she only viewed the body once, refusing to visit the room ever again or attend her son's funeral." Mr. Redding paused. The lights in the room seemed to dim. "After his death, Mary held séances, calling out to her dead son and inviting him to return. He seems to have heard the call, as Mary reported regularly waking up to find Willie standing at the foot of her bed."

Mr. Redding finished. Complete silence had fallen over the class. "Of course, that story is not exactly what we would consider history." His wrinkled face broke into a smile. "But Mary Lincoln certainly believed it."

Sam raised his hand.

"Yes, Mr. West. Do you have any thoughts on our friendly specter?"

Sam had never raised his hand in class before, but what if Mr. Redding had answers? Something that would help him

214

be with Pa. True, Pa wasn't exactly a ghost, but Sam was getting desperate. "Do you believe in ghosts?"

Every eye returned to Mr. Redding, waiting. He took a moment to smooth out his sweater vest. "Belief is a funny thing, isn't it?" He turned to look out the window, his gaze drifting toward the hill, now bathed in afternoon sun. "Notice that you didn't ask me whether ghosts are real, which is a different question altogether, and one I couldn't answer. You asked do I believe in ghosts. The real question then, the true question, is: Do I want to believe?"

His milky gaze settled on Sam. Somehow his eyes were sad and happy at the same time. "Belief is just that. A choice. If you were Mary Todd Lincoln, a grieving mother who had just lost her son, who feared that she'd go the rest of her life and never see him again, what would you choose to believe?"

Mr. Redding waited, like he was expecting an answer. To Sam's surprise, he was saved by Joey Dunkirk.

"You're just avoiding the question. He asked what you believe."

Mr. Redding leaned against the edge of his desk, considering. He wore a gold band on one wrinkly finger and he turned it round and round while he decided how to answer. "Quite right, Mr. Dunkirk, so here's my answer. I want to believe. I really do." Before anyone could ask what he meant, the bell rang and the sound of scraping chair legs and zipping backpacks filled the space between Sam and Mr. Redding.

Suddenly, Sam's heart was beating its way up his throat, and he forgot all about Willie Lincoln's ghost. Mr. Redding might think ghosts were something people imagined, but Pa was real, and he was waiting.

Without hesitation, Sam made his way to the door. He hadn't come up with any excuse to tell Edie, but if he moved fast enough—

"And where do you think you're going?" Edie blocked his path, arms crossed. "And don't say the bathroom."

His brain was working overtime, and for once it surprised him by coming up with a response that wasn't total grape soda. "I left something in my locker."

"All right then, I'll go with you."

Great. "I'll just be a second."

Edie gave him a hard look and then relaxed. "Fine. One second."

"Thanks."

He ran. Sure, it probably looked suspicious, but his mission was too important, even if it meant that Edie might never talk to him again. He pushed his way through the kids in the hallway and made it to the back door in record time.

"Hey, you can't go out that way! Emergency exit!" A

janitor called after him, but he was already outside and running for the hill.

He didn't hear the door open and close behind him.

3:47 p.m.

This time, he didn't see any sign of dragonflies as he approached the tree, just dry bark and bare grass and dead, rattling leaves. He thrust his hand inside, but his knuckles came out scratched and bleeding.

No.

This wasn't happening. It couldn't be closed up already.

He squeezed his head into the darkness, but the hollow didn't stretch around him like before. Splinters scraped his cheek. Before he knew what was happening, someone grabbed his shirt, and he swung around, ready to fight the Boy or the cat or whatever creature was trying to keep him away from Pa, but it was Edie. Her eyes red, probably from the whipping wind.

"What are you doing out here? You promised."

"Nothing, I—" Except he didn't finish, because he couldn't think of a lie, and why couldn't Edie just go away and leave him alone, because time was running out and Pa was trapped?

"Why were you looking inside that tree anyway?" She moved toward the hollow, and Sam didn't mean to do what he did next, but he needed to make her go away.

"Don't!" He jerked her arm, harder than he intended, and she fell, hitting the ground with a cry of surprise. Her glasses tumbled, striking a rock, and maybe, maybe, they cracked a little, but how was that his fault? How?

She looked up at him like he'd just smacked her in the face, which he hadn't. He hadn't even meant to pull her that hard, but even so, he offered to help her up. She glared at his hand but didn't take it. "What was that?" She stood shakily, examining her broken glasses.

"I didn't . . ." He couldn't come up with an answer, because first of all, what could he say? And second of all, why wouldn't she just go away?

"Are you going to tell me why you're out here? Is this some weird game?"

Part of him wanted to explain, to say something that would make her understand that he didn't mean to hurt her, but what?

"Why did you say you wanted to work together in the first place? What's wrong with you?"

"Nothing. I do want to work together. I—" The wind shook the leaves, and for some reason he thought of shriveled strips of skin all dried out like potato chips. Time was running out. The hollow had to open. It had to. "There's just something I need to do. Something important."

Edie's purple hair slapped her face, turning her cheeks an even brighter shade of red.

"About your dad?" Her face softened for a moment. "Miss J said you might need your space. I get that." She stared down at her hands, rubbing her fingers. "But maybe I can help."

Sam swallowed the lump in his throat. He didn't want to lie, again, and he didn't want to hurt Edie, but he needed her to go back inside. Now.

"Just do the project by yourself, okay? You can still have this." He whipped the check from his back pocket and handed it to Edie.

She took it from him, the thin paper lashing the back of her hand. "You're giving me the money? Are you serious?" She drew in a deep breath, and then threw the check into the wind, where it caught in a tangle of dead branches. "Keep your money! I don't want it!"

"Edie, wait," Sam said in a weak voice as she ran back toward the school building. He watched her until she disappeared inside, but didn't follow.

This was what he'd wanted, what he needed. He was doing this for Pa.

3:52 p.m.

No.

Even if the doorway hadn't already been closed, it would probably be too late now. Sam dug the multitool from his backpack and used the knife to cut into the soft wood at the back of the hollow, gouging out a dozen shallow wounds.

"Let me in!"

He tried the corkscrew next, stabbing again and again at the wood, then the screwdriver, then the scissors, before giving up and throwing the multitool as hard as he could into the wind.

"Come out here, you creepy cat! Whatever you are! You have to let me in!"

Beyond the tree, a shadow moved through the field of dead grass that led up to a small wood. Sam recognized that shadow. He ran, backpack forgotten, the tall blades whipping against his legs, and then his foot struck something solid, and the ground was rushing up to meet him. He hit the dirt, but who cares, because he got back up in an instant to face the shadow.

As he watched, the shadow changed, from the cat to the Boy and then back again, settling on something in between.

"I told you to say goodbye," said the in-between thing, licking the dirt from his fingernails with a long, furry tongue. "Now it's too late. These situations, when they do arise, are never permanent. Merely transitory spaces that exist for a time between worlds."

"Open the doorway." Sam squeezed his fingers into fists to keep them from shaking. "I need to go back."

"Too late, I'm afraid. I don't make the rules. I am merely here to assist." He stopped licking his grape-soda hand and watched Sam with not one but two silvery eyes. Unlike before, he wasn't smiling.

"Help me, then."

"As I said, once the door is closed—"

"I know, there's no going back again. But you can open it. And don't lie and say you can't." All around, the world had stopped, no wind, no sound, every blade of grass frozen midsway. "One more day, that's all I need."

The Boy narrowed his eyes, and Sam could see his face reflected in their glassy surface. "To say goodbye?"

"Fine." Sam clenched his jaw, forcing out the words. "To say goodbye."

The Boy twisted his ragged tail between his fingers, considering. "Very well. The hollow will open again tomorrow, 3:45 p.m. You will have five minutes."

Sam's throat seized up at his words, and he couldn't tell if he was going to cry or choke. He opened his mouth to answer, but the world suddenly started up again, wind rushing, children shouting, grass slashing at his legs, and the Boy was gone.

16

SAM RETURNED TO THE TREE, staring into the shadowy center of the hollow. One more day. He had no plan, no way to rescue Pa, but he knew one thing for certain. He also had no intention of saying goodbye. He gathered up his things, the multitool, the duct tape, and the waterproof matches that had slipped out of his pack.

"I called your aunt to pick you up."

Sam turned to find Mr. Redding, his stringy white hair dancing in the wind. Suddenly his argument with Edie rushed back to him, and he felt a pang in the pit of his stomach.

"What about—?"

"She decided to walk."

"Oh."

"Friends, Mr. West. When you're old like me, you know how rare they are. The good ones, at least. Do you want some advice?"

"Not really."

"Fair enough."

He started to walk away from Mr. Redding, but then

sighed. Turned back. "Why are you here, anyway?"

"I am responsible for you, young man," Mr. Redding said, looking down at Sam's hands. "You're bleeding. What happened out here? Anything you want to tell me?"

"Fell, I guess."

"You guess?"

Sam shrugged.

"Well, if there is ever anything you need to talk about, I'm always here." Mr. Redding frowned a while longer at Sam's hands before turning back to the road. "I've got a first-aid kit in my desk, if you—"

"No, thanks."

"At least let me get you a Band-Aid."

"I'm fine. It's just a scratch."

"Fair enough," he repeated.

They turned to face the gravel road. The wind picked up, sending that cloud of white bone dust blossoming on the horizon.

"I told your aunt I'd wait with you, so looks like you're stuck with me a while longer."

"You don't have to."

"No, but here I am."

Behind them, the branches of the dead tree snapped and clicked in the wind. Silence settled between them, and it wasn't a comfortable silence, like with Pa, or the other kind of silence, like when Aunt Jo had come to pick him up. It was another kind of silence altogether.

"But really. Have you ever seen a ghost?" Sam said, because he still hadn't gotten a straight answer.

Mr. Redding twisted his ring some more, and Sam noticed how his hands were so old and wrinkled they reminded him of gator scales.

"Why do you think Willie came back to see Mary Lincoln?" Mr. Redding said, eyes staring at the cloud of rising dust. "Assuming you believe he did."

"That's not an answer."

"I'm just curious."

Sam thought about Mary Lincoln waking up and finding her dead son standing at the foot of her bed. It was a grape-soda question. "Because he missed her. Why else would he come back?"

"But he was dead. Why not stay that way?"

"I told you, because he missed her."

"But what was he, really? Even if we believe this, even if we want to believe more than anything else? What was he? A shadow, an echo, a ghost? A fading memory that couldn't touch or speak or affect anything around him? Have you considered that, Mr. West? All he could do was watch. Not much of a life, if you ask me."

Sam thought back to that awful night with Pa, the way he'd fallen apart minutes after they'd stepped back into this world, the way all the pain of the accident had returned.

But Pa hadn't been a ghost, had he? Besides, it wasn't the same. This was Pa, not some dead kid from a million years ago.

"How do you know what it was like for him? You're not that old."

"No, Mr. West. I'm not that old," Mr. Redding said, sounding almost amused. "I'm asking you. Why would Willie Lincoln choose to stay?"

"For her, his mom. She asked for him."

"She missed him?"

"Of course she did. He was her son," Sam said, the heat building in his chest. "Who wouldn't miss their own son?"

"She couldn't let him go."

"Why should she let go?" Sam's voice had grown louder, angrier, but he didn't care. "It wasn't fair the way he died. Why should she have to let him go?"

"You're right. It was her choice. She chose to believe that Willie was still with her because the alternative . . ."

Mr. Redding took off his ring and examined it in the light. The sun swam across the golden surface, forming a tiny ocean of gently rolling waves. He drew in a deep breath and returned the ring to his finger.

"I don't know anything for certain. There is so little certainty to be had in this world, but I know that sometimes when people die, we have to let them go. Not stop loving them, not forget about them. Just let them go." His eyes suddenly looked faraway, like he was remembering something painful from a long time ago. "If you were Willie Lincoln, what would you want?"

"What do you mean?" Sam said, his anger churning in his stomach.

"For your mother to spend her life in the shadows talking to ghosts? Or for her to live?"

Sam wanted to punch Mr. Redding, because what the heck did he know about anything? Willie Lincoln was different. Pa wasn't even a ghost, not really. He could think and feel and touch. Then again, maybe Willie Lincoln had been like that too once, only he'd stayed in the real world too long. No. No way. Besides, it didn't matter, because Pa couldn't stay, not if it meant he had to die all over again, and Sam wasn't giving up on life. He just wanted to live it with Pa, and where did Mr. Redding get off saying he was wrong? Maybe Mr. Redding should just shut up and stop talking before—

"I believe your ride is here, Mr. West."

Sam hadn't noticed the sound of tires crunching over gravel. Aunt Jo rolled down her window and waved.

"I didn't mention your little excursion this afternoon to your aunt, but I trust you'll consider what I said. About friendship."

"You still haven't told me if you believe in ghosts."

"Didn't I?" Mr. Redding said. "Oh, and promise me you'll do something about those hands." With that, he turned and headed back toward the school. It took every ounce of willpower to stop Sam from running after him and punching that grape-soda mustache right off his grape-soda face.

"What happened to you?" Aunt Jo said as soon as he got in the car. She made him turn his hands over and show her both sides, even though it was just a few scrapes and, what was he, some crybaby?

"I tripped. It was no big deal."

"Jesus, Mary, and Joseph, you call that a few scrapes? You keep this up, you'll be nothing but bandages. Just like your pa. If there was something to trip over within a mile radius, he'd be sure to find it." She shook her head and started up the incline. Clifton Chenier was crooning from the speakers, and Sam recognized Pa's favorite song, "The Cat's Dreamin'." He wondered if she was playing it just for him, or if maybe Pa's tastes were starting to rub off.

Back at the house, Aunt Jo ordered Sam to sit down at the kitchen table so she could wrap his hands, again. She heated up two mugs full of turkey chili, the canned kind, but it was still pretty good, and they ate with the sound of the fridge humming in the background. The really annoying thing was, now that Sam knew tomorrow was his last day here—it had to be—he felt kind of sad leaving Aunt

Jo behind. Even her grape-soda house and her ugly yellow kitchen and the chipped mugs she used as dinner plates no longer seemed so bad.

He didn't know how, but he *was* leaving it all behind. He wouldn't be like Mary Todd Lincoln, asking her son to come back, despite the pain, and turn into some kind of faded-out specter. He'd go with Pa; he'd find a way.

"You done?" Aunt Jo said, offering to take Sam's cup.

"Sure."

"What's all that, anyway?" Sam said when they were done washing and drying the dishes, nodding at the ten white boxes stacked up on the counter.

"Donuts for tonight. We've got meetings here three times a week, four during the holidays. You wanna help me set up? Edie can't make it. Said she might be coming down with something. Did she seem okay at school?"

Sam gulped down the last of his Orange Crush. The fizz stung his throat. "She seemed okay to me."

"But if your hands still hurt, you just say the word. Come to think of it, you'd better rest up. Leave it to me and the crew."

"No, it's okay. I can help." Even though his head was still throbbing, even though he had ghosts swimming around inside his brain and he didn't know what to do about Pa, he thought helping might take his mind off things. Besides, if this really was his last night with Aunt Jo, he'd better make the best of it. He tried not to think about Edie, and how she'd probably never speak to him again, and how her not speaking to him would last forever, because she'd be here and he'd be on the other side with Pa.

Sam started to get up, but Aunt Jo shook her head. "No, siree. You sit down and rest those hands. You'll be on donut duty."

Aunt Jo got out cups and napkins, and then headed to the living room to start on the folding chairs.

"I thought I told you to rest," Aunt Jo said as Sam followed her into the living room.

"I did. All better."

Aunt Jo frowned, but she let Sam help her drag the chairs out of the closet, and together they set up over twenty of them, shoved in here and there, wherever they would fit.

"Does it ever hurt?" Sam said, as he helped Aunt Jo scoot the couch back so they could squeeze in a few more chairs. He was impressed by how easily she moved stuff around, like it didn't even matter that one of her legs was made of metal.

Aunt Jo didn't have to ask what he was talking about. "Sure it does. If you ever see me pucker up my face like I just swallowed a lemon, you can bet it's my leg."

"What did it feel like when it happened?"

"That should just about do it," she said, grabbing the last three chairs all at once and handing one to Sam. "Apart from hurting like heck, it felt . . . unreal. Like I couldn't believe the rest of my leg was missing." They finished and then Aunt Jo plopped down on the couch, Sam sinking into the spot beside her. "Strange thing was, it was my foot that hurt the worst. You know, phantom pains? And it wasn't just a tickle or an itch, it was straight-up pain. I used to stay up nights wondering how something that wasn't even there could hurt so bad."

"But it's not so bad anymore?"

"Not most of the time, but I still have those nights. At first I thought I'd never get used to having a big hunk of plastic rubbing against my skin." She tapped on the top of her prosthetic leg. It almost sounded hollow. "I was sure my life was over, full stop, that was it."

"So what happened? How'd you move on?"

There was a knock on the door. Aunt Jo stood up with a groan. "I kept going. One day at a time. Every day got a little easier. Of course, I had dark times too—that's why we're here—but I kept at it." She ignored the knocking for a moment and her eyes met Sam's. "I'll never get my leg back, not the way it used to be, but all in all, life's good. It's not the way I expected, but I can live with it."

He heard more cars pull up the drive. The knocking got louder. She pulled Sam into a hug, and this time he hugged her back.

Edie didn't show up that night, even though Sam had secretly hoped she might, and so he was on his own. He served donuts and washed dishes and listened to people's stories. No matter where they were in their journeys, the speakers all sounded a lot like Aunt Jo. According to them, it was all about taking it one day at a time and keeping on, even when you'd rather dig yourself a hole and go hide in it.

One speaker, a lady with huge gold earrings shaped like lions, said how she'd accidentally set her house on fire by falling asleep on the couch with a lit cigarette, and how that had been the worst day of her life, because it was the day she hit rock bottom. But it was also the best day, because her house burned down and it meant she had no choice but to start from scratch. Door closed. No going back.

When the speakers were done talking and mingling, and Sam finally had the kitchen spotless, he headed upstairs, leaving Aunt Jo behind to see out the last of her guests. He closed the door to his room and collapsed on the bed, head buzzing with questions.

He thought about what Mr. Redding had said about Mary and Willie Lincoln. Had Willie come back because he wanted to, or because Mary wouldn't let him go? Did it even matter? Pa couldn't come back, not like that, which meant Sam wasn't the one holding on. Besides, maybe Mr. Redding had it wrong. Maybe it wasn't just Mary who'd been clinging too tight to the past, but both of them. Maybe they both wanted life to go back to the way it had been.

What was so bad about that?

And he wasn't asking Pa to stay. He was going. He thought about Aunt Jo downstairs, and about Edie. Was he selfish for leaving without bothering to explain? Was he giving up his life like Mr. Redding had said? Then an even worse thought crept in. What if he couldn't leave? What if there wasn't a way for him to stay with Pa, and the Boy was right? What if he went back through the hollow tomorrow and had no choice but to say goodbye?

Despite the war raging in his head, he fell asleep almost immediately. When he woke up again, it was still dark out. He went to the window and eased it open, letting the cool night air wash across his face, looking for the source of the noise that had woken him up. The maple stood tall and proud in the middle of the backyard. Its green leaves seemed to glow a fiery orange in the moonlight. In the distance, a column of smoke rose up toward the stars, and he could hear sirens. Were they heading to someone's house? Or maybe a forest fire?

A strong gust shook the maple, and he blinked the sting from his eyes. He could smell the smoke now, taste the bitter air on his tongue.

He watched the smoke for a while as it reached up to the bottom of the clouds, and he couldn't help thinking back to the woman with lion earrings. After the house fire, she'd had no choice but to start from scratch. It was like the fire had erased her old life, giving her a fresh start.

The sirens faded, and he spotted a halo of orange flames lighting a single spot on the horizon. Even though they must have been miles away, if he squinted, it was like those flames were enveloping the largest branch of Aunt Jo's maple.

The wind picked up, making his eyes water, but he didn't care. Suddenly, he found himself laughing. It was so simple. Leaving the window open, he returned to bed. Even though he was exhausted, he couldn't stop smiling, because he knew now how he could stay with Pa.

17

EDIE DIDN'T SIT BY HIM on the bus the next morning. Instead she headed all the way to the back and disappeared in a sea of raincoats and umbrellas. It had started raining again just after breakfast—jelly-filled donuts and a sip of Aunt Jo's coffee—and Aunt Jo said it was set to rain so much for the next few days that Noah would have felt right at home. According to her, that was a Holler, Oklahoma, first.

In class, they watched a documentary about the Civil War. Usually, Sam would want to know everything, like how the soldiers survived with no shelter or food or medicine—answer: they mostly didn't—but he had bigger questions on his mind. Like what would Aunt Jo think when she came to pick him up after school and he wasn't there? Would Edie hate him for the rest of her life, or would she forget about him? Like he'd never existed, and why did he even care?

He looked over at Edie, face hidden in her purple hoodie, and an ache sprouted in his chest. What was wrong with him? He hardly even knew her, but the ache kept spreading, like he'd just gotten a shot full of grape soda, and so he swallowed it down again and went back to watching the movie.

Lunch was something called tuna-mac surprise. The surprise was that it had crunchy onions on top, which, by the way, didn't actually qualify as a surprise. Also, gross. Sam pulled on his hoodie and sat in his usual spot in the courtyard. Even though he was the only one there, because it was raining, and it was a total grape-soda move to sit outside, he wished Edie would join him. Even if she was basically a stranger and after today he'd never see her again. And so what? It didn't matter.

Edie didn't sit with him at lunch.

He saw her later coming out of the girls' bathroom, and he wondered if maybe she'd been sitting in there the whole time. She pretended not to see him. Sam had the sudden urge to run after her and say something, anything, but he didn't.

After lunch, they learned about what winter was like for the Civil War soldiers. Answer: not very good. They would settle into winter camps where they were lucky to get a few potatoes or onions for dinner. To them, tuna-mac surprise would have been like heaven. Since conditions were too bad for fighting, they had to find ways to pass the time, like card games, chores, or storytelling.

Sam thought of Pa when he saw the grainy black-and-white photos of men gathered around campfires telling tales. If Pa had been alive back then, he would have been the best storyteller of them all.

He thought back to Mama and the journals and how upset he'd been that Pa hadn't told him the whole truth about his life. Now, hopefully, he'd have all the time in the world to find out.

The rain that had died down for a bit that afternoon started up again, battering the windows and making several people sit up straighter in their seats. When the bell rang, Sam stuffed his notebook and pencils into his backpack and checked his other supplies. He was ready, and he didn't have to worry about Edie following him, which was good, but it also made him sad. He looked over at her desk to see if she was staying late, but all he saw was her purple hair disappearing around the corner.

3:43 p.m.

Time to go.

"Staying late again, Mr. West?" Mr. Redding came over and leaned on Sam's desk.

"No, sir. I was just leaving."

"I see."

Sam could feel Mr. Redding watching him as he turned to go.

236

"Be careful, Mr. West," Mr. Redding called as Sam hurried into the hallway. "I'm always here if you need to talk."

A sheet of rain slapped Sam's face as soon as he opened the back door. Tightening his grip on his backpack, he took a deep breath and made a run for it. The wind howled, trying to blow him off track, but he pushed forward, rain pellets stinging his face, streaking his vision.

The Boy had given him five minutes. He had to hurry.

When he reached the tree, dragonflies were pouring out of the hollow just like before, landing in twitching piles on the ground, unable to fly in the fierce wind and rain. He didn't hesitate but scrambled inside, ignoring the crunch of insect bodies and wings. Thick spiderwebs filled the tunnel, glittering in the dim light. They clung to his face and hair as he pushed onward, and this time the other side drew him forward. The tunnel opened up, and suddenly he was falling again, like before. Twisting around tight bends, bombarded by the smell of wet leaves, dense swamp, deep waters. He shivered as creatures with legs as thin as thread skittered down his arms and legs, drawing intricate brushwork patterns across his skin.

As he dropped onto the mossy earth on the other side, a ray of sunlight bathed his face. Through the treetops he could see a blue, cloudless sky. He stood up, and already his sopping wet clothes and hair had started to dry in the afternoon heat. He unzipped his bag and took out his supplies.

No hesitation, because why? Why should he wait? His five minutes were already running out. This was for Pa, so they could be together, and what did it matter if he left a few people he barely knew behind?

He took out the small bottle of lighter fluid and laid it on the grass, next to the plastic box containing waterproof matches. The tools he would need to complete his plan.

This was it.

Now or never.

An image of Aunt Jo flitted into his mind, as she sat in her car waiting for him to come back, the sky growing dark around her, reaching for her phone but not knowing who to call. An image of Edie sitting in class, looking over at his desk day after day, wondering.

He shook his head, pushing the unwanted images aside. Drawing in a deep breath, he opened the bottle of lighter fluid and soaked the hollow and the base of the tree. The smell of it clung to the inside of his nostrils. When he tore off the first match his hand was shaking.

This was it.

A weak flame sputtered to life, growing stronger in the breeze.

No choice but to start from scratch. Doorway closed. No going back.

He dropped the match inside the hollow, and the flame flared instantly and spread down the trunk. He lit another match and dropped it next to the first, and another. Soon the hollow was alive with fire.

He watched it burn for a moment, pushing away all the doubts creeping in at the edges of his mind, and then he found the canoe and rode across the tranquil green waters to the other side. Instead of stopping at the dock, the canoe continued on to the small beach beside the white house. It slid up onto the sandy shore, and there was Pa, waiting to greet him.

"Pa!" Sam climbed out of the canoe, and Pa ran to meet him. Sam squeezed him tight, his body reassuringly solid, and he breathed in his scent, bait and cigarette smoke and motor oil.

"I thought you were gone for good," Pa said, and Sam could tell from the look on his face that he was trying not to cry, because of the way he was working his lips back and forth and clenching his jaw.

"I'm back, Pa. For good this time. I figured out a way we can be together."

Pa's gaze drifted over Sam's shoulder, where a column of gray smoke rose above the treetops. Pa scrunched up his forehead in confusion.

"It was the only way. The Boy, the cat, whatever he is, told me himself. Once the doorway's closed, there's no going back. And this is the last day. He sent me here to say goodbye."

Pa took a step away from Sam, peering at the rising smoke.

"But I don't have to say goodbye. I figured it out. If there is no doorway, that means he can't send me back. I can stay here with you. Forever." The word *forever* caught in Sam's throat.

Pa looked like Sam had just punched him in the face. He placed a rough hand on Sam's cheek, staring straight into his eyes. He could tell Pa didn't understand.

"It's a good thing. It'll work this time, I promise, and I won't have to leave you, and everything can go back to the way it should be."

Overhead, the sunlight had already started to fade, casting long shadows over the beach.

In the dying light, Pa's skin flickered, and for a moment Sam could see straight through to his bones and organs and the tangled grass on the other side.

"Pa? Did you hear me? Everything's going to be all right."

Pa's face split into a sad smile, and then it crumpled, almost like he was in pain.

"What is it?" Sam said. "Does it hurt?"

Pa shook his head, tearing his eyes away from Sam. "No, it's not that." The flames had breached the tree line, and Pa watched them for a second as they licked the belly of the low-hanging clouds. "You can't stay here. Not for good.

Not like this." The words caught in his throat, but he forced them out. "You have to go back."

Sam couldn't believe what he was hearing. "You don't know what you're saying," Sam said. "We won. I found a way."

"I'm dead, Sammy." Pa looked at him again, and it was almost like he was scared of his own words. "But you're not."

"No! You don't get it. We can be together now. You and me. This doesn't have to be the end."

"Sam, please. Don't make this harder than it already is." Pa looked down at his hands. As the sunlight faded, so did Pa. Sam reached out, but his hand passed right through.

"No!" Sam shouted. "This can't be happening. I figured it out. Pa . . ." Sam grasped Pa's arm again, but it was no use. He couldn't get ahold of him. Like he was disappearing right before Sam's eyes. Like he was . . . a ghost.

For a moment, Pa smiled. His same crooked smile, full of missing teeth and a whole lot of mischief. All around, the sky grew dark, shadows creeping across the water. A breeze blew over the sand, bringing with it the sting of smoke.

"You have to go back," Pa said, his voice a bruise, his words flickering in and out right along with his body. "Go back for me."

A wave of anger swept through Sam's chest, and suddenly he wished Pa was solid again so he could hit him.

"I did this for you," he said, gesturing toward the burning tree. "I'm staying for you!"

"I know." Pa let his hand hover over Sam's shoulder, but Sam could no longer feel his touch. "And you can do this for me too."

"Shut up, Pa," Sam spat. But before Pa could respond, they felt a vibration under their feet.

Behind them, on the dirt road leading from the house down to the beach, a car revved its engine. Tires crunched over rocks and sand, and a pair of headlights roared to life, trapping Sam and Pa in two blazing white beams.

"Pa, look out!" The memory of his previous visit rushed back to him, and Sam knew on instinct that the lights were his enemy. They meant to take Pa away from him. The engine revved louder, and Sam tried but failed to take Pa's hand.

Sam ordered Pa to move back, toward the water and the waiting canoe, but Pa refused to budge. He just stood there and watched as his '68 Pontiac Sunbird lumbered forward, bumping over rocks and sand, before pulling to a stop not a foot away from Pa, her nose kissing the murky water. The doors on either side swung open, and the headlights flared, casting the swamp in an eerie green glow, and there, sitting in the driver's seat was One-Eye. He blinked his silvery eye.

"Pa, come on! We have to get out of here!" Sam swiped

at Pa, lashing out, but he couldn't grab hold. He watched, helpless, as One-Eye shivered and changed from a cat to a boy and finally to a familiar woman with long dark hair and a smile Sam had only seen once, the day she died.

"Ma?" Sam said. Ma's smile widened, and she waved, and she was glowing inside too, like she had a ball of fireflies buzzing away inside her chest.

"I'm sorry, Sammy, but I think that's my ride," Pa said, turning around to face Sam. "I know what you did for me, what you tried to do, but it's not your time."

"Shut up! Stop talking!"

"I know. I never was much good at talking unless I was telling a story." Pa's face crumpled again, but then he regained control, took a deep breath. "Don't know why I died when I did, and I don't know if there's any meaning to it. I wish I could change it so much, but I can't. We can't. You have to go out there and live your life. I've had my stories. I've lived them. Well, except for the ones I made up."

Pa smiled again, but Sam couldn't take it. "Stop it. Just . . . stop."

"It's time for you to go out there and make your own stories, Sammy. Bigger and better ones. There are people counting on you now. And, one day, when you have your own kid, you can tell them all about me. And, more important, you can tell them all about you. About the stories you've made. You're a West, Sammy. You're meant to live wild. Go out there and wrestle a few dozen rattlesnakes for me."

"Pa, don't," Sam said, deflating a little more with each word.

Ma scooted over, and Pa climbed into the driver's seat, ignoring the dragonflies, each the size of model airplanes, that had gathered on the dash. "I know you didn't want to say goodbye, so we won't." Pa swallowed, and for a minute it was like he was choking, but then he caught his breath. "I love you, son."

"Pa . . ." Sam's throat hurt, and he wanted to scream and fight and drag Pa out of the car, but he couldn't. He couldn't do anything but watch as Pa laid his foot on the gas pedal and revved the engine. The car lurched back, away from the water, and Pa held up his hand. Sam told himself he wouldn't. He wouldn't wave goodbye, because this wasn't goodbye, it couldn't be.

Then the water exploded behind him, soaking Sam and Pa and Ma and the Sunbird in a spray of dark water. Sam watched in amazement as the Colonel emerged slowly from the swamp and, with a little encouragement from Pa, crawled into the back seat. He could only fit if he coiled up his tail and sat with his front legs hanging out the window, but he fit, and, like Pa, his body had started to fade. As soon as the Colonel was settled inside, the car doors snapped shut and a new light opened in the sky back in the direction of the house.

It was so bright, it was like someone had torn a hole in the shadows and revealed a new sun. Pa lifted his hand again. Despite the pain throbbing in Sam's face and the voice in his head shouting for it all to stop, to change, for Pa not to go, Sam lifted his hand too.

Pa slid the gearshift into drive, and the car shot forward. He braked at the edge of the yard, hand still raised. Sam could barely see him now through the blinding sunlight, his flickering form mixing in with the surrounding rays, but he could tell Pa was smiling.

He revved the engine one last time, and then the Sunbird took off, heading directly for the center of the light. The light grew brighter and brighter, throbbing and pulsing, until Sam had to bury his head in his hands. That grape-soda light burned his eyes and he couldn't believe what was happening and he couldn't do a single thing to stop it. Then, with a snap, the light disappeared and Pa and the Sunbird and everything Sam had ever cared about were gone.

18

SAM RAN TO THE FRONT yard, to the spot where the light had been, and he stood alone in the darkness, a cool breeze blowing the grass at his feet. He dropped to the ground, ignoring the smoke stinging his eyes and the echo of Pa's words.

Pa had abandoned him.

He wanted Sam to go back, to live his life, but what was the point?

Feet heavy as stones, he walked to the shore, kicking at the sand, gouging out holes that filled with dirty water. The canoe bobbed up and down just a few feet away.

He wouldn't go back. He couldn't—he'd made sure of that. But Pa was gone and, even as he watched, the house started to fade. The glow of the fire lit up the weathered dock, the dirty white siding, the beer-can chimes clinking gently in the wind. It all shimmered and rippled, becoming less and less solid, until he could see the trees and the road and the tangle of bushes on the other side. Then even those started to fade.

Hands shaking, still telling himself he would never leave,

he climbed into the canoe, and it launched forward, cutting a clean path through the water. He looked back, and the house was barely a shimmer, a million glittering particles, like water droplets, slowly floating apart from one another, until he couldn't see a house or a dock or a shore, but a spray of silver stars. Then even the stars winked out, and the house was gone, and the shore and the swamp, and all that remained was a cool, empty blackness.

The canoe hit the sand, and Sam lurched forward, tumbling over the edge. He stood, walking into the smoke, and there was the tree, his tree, swallowed in rising flames. They billowed from the center of the hollow like a dragon breathing fire, and even though Pa was gone, his voice urged him forward.

"Go, Sammy! Hurry!"

He moved closer, eyes watering, the heat washing over him in waves. He wouldn't go, he couldn't. The flames would devour him alive, and then . . .

"Trust me. Go now!"

He couldn't. He wouldn't leave.

And yet, as if he had no control over it, he took another step forward. Then another. With each step, the heat singed his skin. Pain radiated up his bare arms, his face. He was burning.

Sam dropped to his knees at the base of the tree, reaching up into the flames. This was it. He was going to die here, alone, a failure. Stuck in a world of perpetual darkness. His skin bubbled, and each of the bubbles burst and shriveled, turning to ash as he sat and watched. This was it. It was over.

He sank back, and that was when he saw a hand reach through from the other side. It couldn't be—it wasn't possible—but he recognized the chipped purple nail polish.

He grasped the hand, ignoring the flames eating away at his skin, and then, as suddenly as before, he was flying. Vines slashed his face and spiderwebs filled his mouth, but he kept flying, and the whole way he was crying and screaming out for Pa and then, with a splash, he hit the ground and found himself flat on his back in the middle of a mud puddle.

"Sam!" He blinked, head throbbing, skin burning, and suddenly Edie was there, hugging him tight. "What happened? Where have you been?"

He felt his face and hands and arms, searching for signs of fire, of scorched and bubbling skin, but it was like none of it had ever happened. The world came back into focus. He looked up at the angry gray sky and saw that, apart from a light mist, the rain had stopped.

"How did you . . . ?" Sam started, his throat hoarse. He wanted to yell at Edie because she'd brought him back, but here she was, and he wanted her to keep hugging him and he wanted Pa and he wanted everything to be true all at once, but now he knew it couldn't be. Edie let him go and sat back on the grass.

"I started to walk home, but I was worried about you." She looked at him, then looked away, then looked at him again. He had this strange tingling in his chest, and he didn't know what it meant, but maybe it felt okay.

He could tell she wanted to ask him a million questions, like why he kept running off and how he'd gotten trapped in a tree that clearly wasn't big enough to fit him, but instead she just sat there, and he sat there, and they didn't say anything, but it was the comfortable kind of silence, like when he was out fishing with Pa.

They watched some birds splash in a nearby puddle for a while, and it was strange, because Sam had lost everything he'd ever cared about, but part of him felt like smiling. A small part, but still.

"Thanks for coming to get me."

"No problem. Rescuing people from man-eating trees is kind of my specialty."

"Really?"

"It's a new specialty. You may or may not be the first."

"Right." He smiled, even though he didn't want to smile, and they watched as the clouds parted and the sun stained the sky a pale shade of purple. "Sorry about the science fair. I didn't mean what I said before. Any of it."

"It's okay. I figured you were probably going through

some stuff. I should have given you more space."

"Nah, I was a jerk."

"Maybe a little." Now Edie smiled, a half smile, kind of like Pa's, and then she went back to watching the sky. They sat there until the next round of rain came in, and it was the kind that came in sudden and fast. The kind where the sky opened and dropped a solid curtain of raindrops, each as big as your fist.

"Run!" Edie shouted, and she didn't need to tell him twice. They ran. And despite everything that had happened, leaving Pa behind, his bruised body, his burning skin, it turned into a race. Edie won for a while, and then Sam pushed ahead and, by the time they made their way inside, Edie inching out the win, they were both laughing. It didn't even matter that their shoes squeaked and that they both slipped at the same time on the wet tile.

"I see you made it back," Mr. Redding said, helping Edie and then Sam off the ground.

They went to his classroom to wait for Aunt Jo, and Mr. Redding made them powdered hot cocoa with tiny marshmallows, which wasn't Orange Crush, but was still pretty good. They sipped their drinks and looked out the window and watched the rain wash away all the dirt and dust.

"Will I see you two after school tomorrow?" Mr. Redding said, a curious expression on his face.

Sam glanced at Edie, who winked. Sam said, "Looks

like." And even though his heart was aching, even though every ounce of him would have gone with Pa if he could have, it was nice. A strange calm had settled over him, like the feeling he'd gotten at the end of the hundred-yard dash. And even though he'd lost, even though every bit of his energy hadn't been enough, he was still here, and maybe that was something.

Aunt Jo arrived in a bright green poncho that made her look like a giant praying mantis. "Jesus, Mary, and Joseph, look at you two. I thought you were building planes, not taking swimming lessons." Edie looked at Sam, who shrugged.

"We tried to do a test flight," Edie said. "Bad timing."

"And you being under the weather." Aunt Jo shook her head at Edie. "Come on, you little hellions. Let's get you warmed up. Mr. Redding, these two cause you any trouble?" She chatted a while with Mr. Redding before they all headed out. "How about we stop by Gina's Diner on the way home?" Aunt Jo said as they squeaked their way down the hall. "I heard she's serving her famous lava cake this week."

"Lava cake?" Sam said.

"It's pretty amazing," Edie said. They got ready to run to Baby Girl, Edie and Sam using their backpacks as umbrellas. "It's a red velvet cake with bubbly melted fudge inside, and it spills out when you cut into it just like real lava, so you have to eat it really fast."

"What do you say?" Aunt Jo said, looking over at Sam and wiggling her eyebrows.

This was it. The doorway was closed, and Pa was gone, and he wanted to go home, but Aunt Jo kept looking at him, waiting, and Edie looked over at him too, and he had that weird tingling in his chest, and he wasn't hungry, but he opened the door, letting in a gust of wind and rain and said, "Sounds good. Who wants to race?"

They picked up lava cake and fried catfish with a side of pickles for Edie, and they ate on Aunt Jo's couch watching *Young Frankenstein*, which was Edie's favorite movie. Edie's mom came to pick her up around nine, and even though Sam didn't see her, he heard her and Aunt Jo talking for a long time out on the porch.

When they were gone, he went upstairs and lay down on his bed, watching the shadowy maple branches dance outside his window. It was raining again, and even though he could hear the raindrops pattering against the glass, he could also feel the quiet. A new kind of quiet that settled on his chest, pressing him down into the mattress. The walls closed in around him, like the sides of an invisible coffin, and despite Edie and the lava cake and Aunt Jo, he'd never felt so alone.

❌ ❌ ❌

That Saturday, Aunt Jo offered to take him fishing, and he wanted to say no, but then Edie was coming, too, and he just sort of went along with it. Aunt Jo knew a lot about fishing, just like Pa. She spent the ride down to the lake telling them about her favorite lures and about the time Pa had hooked a giant catfish and it had dragged him halfway across Sardis Lake. Sam had heard that story before too, but not the part about Pa getting pulled from the boat and coming up with his pants around his ankles.

Another detail Pa had neglected to tell him.

They parked by this huge concrete dam and walked on down to the lake. The beach was made of weeds and rocks and mostly dead grass, not a single speck of sand.

"Ain't she a sight?" Aunt Jo said, peering out at the muddy lake, and Sam didn't answer, because he was too busy eyeing all the trash that people had left on the so-called beach: beer cans, a half-empty Coke bottle, a used diaper, a pack of hot dogs with the pink juice still floating in the bottom.

Even with the dumpy beach, fishing wasn't all that bad. Edie had never fished before, and so Sam showed her how to bait her hook and cast her reel, and she caught the first fish, a spotted bass weighing in at just over five pounds.

"Guess you had a good teacher," Sam said, and Edie punched his arm, harder than necessary, but it still made him laugh.

After a few more hours of sweating and waiting, without

the faintest hint of shade, Sam was ready to call it quits, but Aunt Jo said to give it a few more minutes. Sam hadn't caught anything worth keeping yet, and his head ached. He closed his eyes and imagined he was back home, drifting down Ol' Tired Eyes, Pa at his side, the muggy heat broken up by long stretches of shade.

That was when he felt the first tug. It was a big tug, too, and so he sat up straighter and tugged right back. Hard, but not hard enough to break the line.

"That's it. Slow and steady," Aunt Jo said, searching the still water for any sign of movement. "Told you it'd be worth the wait."

Sam reeled in his line nice and easy, the tension building, until soon he was on his feet.

"You got yourself a fighter," Aunt Jo said, and she was right, because just then Sam's rod jerked, the force of it dragging him to the edge of the boat. "Hold on!" Aunt Jo said, grabbing at the back of his shirt, but it was too late. His rod jerked again, and the next thing he knew he was plunging into the muddy water.

He made the mistake of opening his mouth, and the dirty water rushed in. Arms flailing, he sank deeper into the cloudy depths, and he might have drowned if that same tug hadn't come again, this time pulling on his wrist, and he realized that he'd forgotten to let go of his rod. That fish, if it really was a fish, dragged him to the surface, where he sputtered and choked and he tried to call out, but there was no time.

WHAM!

With the strength of a dozen sharks, that fish wrenched him into midair and, just like that, he was flying. Not really flying, but it felt like flying, and soon he was skidding across the water just like a dragonfly, zipping and zooming, the spray cooling his sunburned skin, his legs flopping out behind him like a fishtail, only with jeans and boots instead of scales. His brain shouted at his hands to let go of the rod, but he didn't, and so he kept right on zooming. Up ahead, he could just make out a mammoth shape the size of a whale cutting a path through the water, but he knew it couldn't be a whale, which could only mean one thing . . . it must be a catfish! A huge catfish, and that would mean that maybe Pa had been telling the truth about getting dragged across Sardis Lake all those years ago.

"Yahoo!" Sam bellowed, still skidding across the waves, a spray of dirty water battering his face.

The creature picked up speed, and now Sam was really flapping and flying, touching down every once in a while, but mostly keeping airborne. "Whoopee!" he shouted, his voice carrying on the wind, stretching out into one long, jubilant howl.

Then the line broke, and Sam lost his grip on the rod, but he didn't stop right away. He kept on skidding over the

255

surface of the water, then the skid turned into a roll, and finally he came to a stop on a patch of sandy beach.

Mud might have been a better word, but it was fine and grainy like sand, and as he sat up and looked down at his feet—now bare except for one soggy sock—he saw that he was stepping on a seashell. He picked it up and cleaned out the center and felt around the edges, but didn't find a single crack.

A perfect seashell on a perfect beach, hidden on the world's ugliest lake.

He sat there for a while, watching the water lap at his toes, and he was thinking about everything that had happened, and about Pa's stories, and how maybe it didn't matter so much which parts were true and which were made up. He closed his eyes and pictured how Pa's face would light up if he ever got the chance to tell him about what had just happened. Even though it made him sad, because Pa was gone and probably no one else would believe him, it made him happy too.

He'd been mad at Pa for not always telling him the truth, but maybe he'd been missing the point. Stories were about what had happened, sure, but they were also about what you wanted to believe, and about the parts of your life you wanted to pass on. Maybe Pa hadn't told him about Mama for a reason, because he didn't want Sam to feel guilty. It wasn't because Pa didn't care enough to tell him the truth.

Maybe it was just the opposite.

Aunt Jo showed up after a while, and Edie was the first to jump from the boat. "Oh my god, what happened? Are you okay?"

Sam considered telling her the true story, about being dragged across the lake by a giant catfish, but instead he just smiled. "Here, I found this on the beach." He handed her the shell, and her cheeks turned pink, and then, once Aunt Jo was finished fussing over his scrapes and bruises, they laid out a blanket on the mud that almost looked like sand and had themselves a picnic.

It was a Tuesday around Halloween, about five months after losing Pa, when Sam was called into Mr. Redding's office during lunch. Or, to be more accurate, Principal Redding's office, since he'd recently been promoted. "A funny thing happened today in the teacher's lounge," Mr. Redding said, stroking the tips of his mustache. "Mrs. Lee says she found a bullfrog in her mailbox, and we've had reports of lizards popping up in faculty lunches. Now, you wouldn't know anything about that, would you, Mr. West?"

Mr. Redding's eyes sparkled behind his thick glasses.

"No, sir. Can't say that I do."

"You may remember a story I told you once about your pa and one ornery possum. That's a pretty big coincidence, wouldn't you say? One might even suggest that the two

257

incidents appear connected."

Sam bit back a smile, especially because he'd caught sight of a small green lizard making its way up the edge of Mr. Redding's desk.

"In all seriousness, I'm glad to see that you're settling in here, I really am. But we have rules for a reason." Mr. Redding sighed, giving his chin a scratch. Sam noticed that he was no longer wearing the gold ring he'd had on last year. Instead it hung from a chain around his neck.

"Is that your wife?" Sam said, looking at a picture of a younger Mr. Redding with a kind-looking woman with wild gray curls.

"That is indeed. She passed away a few years ago now. Beverly was her name." He felt the spot on his finger where the ring had been. "She was a teacher here for thirty-two years, and a huge fan of practical jokes." His face split with laughter and his eyes were no longer there with Sam but in another place. "She once lined all the cushions in our house with bubble wrap, under the covers, and every time I sat down I . . ." He had to pause for breath, he was trying so hard not to laugh. "I couldn't figure out why all the cushions kept popping, until I unzipped the covers and looked inside. I ended up calling the police to report a home invader, and that finally got her to confess." Tears squeezed from the sides of his eyes as he gave way to a low, rumbling laugh, and then the laugh turned into a cough, and then it was quiet.

Sam shifted in his chair.

Mr. Redding sat up straighter. "Well, seeing as there's no proof that you had anything to do with the recent incident, I guess you're free to go." He studied Sam's face, and Sam did his best to look innocent. "But I should warn you, Mr. West, that if we have any more unwanted visitors in this school, you may not be so lucky. Understood?"

"Yes, sir," Sam said, trying not to look at the lizard that was now squeezing its way into Mr. Redding's briefcase.

Winter brought ice storms and one good day of snow. Sam was glad to get past it all, especially Thanksgiving and Christmas, and finally make it into spring. It was late March when Sam headed down to the kitchen and stuffed a six-pack of Orange Crush into his backpack along with the De Havilland Mosquito bomber, now freshly painted and glued, with a propeller made from 3D-printed plastic.

"I'll be back in an hour," he called to Aunt Jo, who was slicing up chocolate cake in the kitchen.

"Don't forget, I need you here at six sharp," Aunt Jo said. Sam could smell the freshly cut cake, and he didn't even mind that he had to set up chairs and do a million dishes in exchange for a slice.

Sam met Edie at the corner, and they rode their bikes toward school. They'd bought the bikes from their science fair winnings, along with a new sound system for Aunt Jo and some new clothes for Edie's mom, who had just gotten a job answering phones at a real-estate office downtown.

When the asphalt turned to gravel, they rode on the grass instead, past the school and up the small hill leading to the tree. Bright green leaves had sprouted from its branches a while back, even before the end of winter. The hollow that had once been a scary, gaping mouth now looked like two puckered lips. It had closed up little by little, ever since the day Sam had started the fire. The fire that, by the way, hadn't left a single scorch mark.

Instead, the tree had come alive, and Edie had made a wind chime out of spoons and old soda cans and hung it from the lowest branch. They sat by the tree, the sunlight peeking through the branches, and they each opened up a can of warm Orange Crush. Edie drank first, then Sam, and then Sam opened a third can and poured it on the dry Oklahoma dirt.

He never saw any dragonflies after that spring when he'd said goodbye to Pa. Or any sign of that mangy old cat. Once, he saw a silver glint peeking out at him from beneath a bush, but it turned out to only be a quarter.

"Ready to race?" Edie said, eyes twinkling in the sunlight. "My glider is so going to beat your Mosquito."

"You wish."

They chugged their sodas as fast as they could, until

bubbles spilled out of their noses. Then Edie laughed and Sam laughed too, and he leaned in close, so close he could smell the sweet Orange Crush on Edie's lips, and the wind rustled the maple leaves overhead, and he kept right on leaning.

Acknowledgments

A huge thank-you to everyone who keeps me going. To all the writers, artists, and creators who have inspired me along the way. To my agent, Brianne Johnson, who always has my back and has the coolest, witchiest apartment in the entire universe. To everyone at HarperCollins and Temple Hill for helping this project come to life. And, finally, to all the dreamers who create with wild abandon. Thank you!